CAIN'S JUSTICE

ALSO BY ROBERT VAUGHAN

The Tenderfoot
On the Oregon Trail
Cold Revenge
Iron Horse
Outlaw Justice
Western Fiction Ten Pack

The Founders Series
The Western Adventures of Cade McCall
Faraday Series
Lucas Cain Series
Chaney Brothers Westerns
Arrow and Saber Series
The Crocketts Series
Remington Series

...and many more

CAIN'S JUSTICE

LUCAS CAIN
BOOK FOUR

ROBERT VAUGHAN

WOLFPACK
PUBLISHING
— EST 2013 —

Cain's Justice
Paperback Edition
Copyright © 2024 Robert Vaughan

Wolfpack Publishing
701 S. Howard Ave. 106-324
Tampa, Florida 33609

wolfpackpublishing.com

This book is a work of fiction. Any references to historical events, real people or real places are used fictitiously. Other names, characters, places and events are products of the author's imagination, and any resemblance to actual events, places or persons, living or dead, is entirely coincidental.

All rights reserved. No part of this book may be reproduced by any means without the prior written consent of the publisher, other than brief quotes for reviews.

Paperback ISBN 978-1-63977-367-1
eBook ISBN 978-1-63977-366-4
LCCN 2024932145

CAIN'S JUSTICE

1

The sun dipped below the horizon, casting long shadows across the wide-open spaces of Taylor County, Texas. Riley Baker, Leon Spence, and Muley Carter rode hard, the hooves of their horses beating a rhythm of urgency against the dusty trail. The stagecoach with the dead guard and driver were on the Buffalo Gap Road behind them.

The stolen pouch, containing a meager four hundred dollars, lay heavy in Riley Baker's hands, a cruel reminder of their miscalculation. The tension among the outlaws was palpable, the unspoken understanding that their impulsive act had consequences far beyond their initial expectations.

Baker, the leader of the trio, glanced over his shoulder, his eyes narrowing as he scanned the barren landscape. "We gotta get a move on, boys. The law ain't gonna be far behind, not after what Spence did back there."

Leon Spence, a man with a wild look in his eyes, ran a shaky hand through his disheveled hair. "Four hundred dollars, Riley! We risked our necks for this piddlin' pickin's."

Muley Carter, the youngest of the group, shifted uncomfortably in the saddle. He kept stealing glances at the stolen money, guilt etched on his face. "What if we split up? Head in different directions, throw off anyone tailin' us?"

Baker shook his head. "No, Muley. They'll pick us off one by one. We stand a better chance together. We just need a hideout, someplace where we can catch our breath and figure out our next move. We need to lie low for a while."

"Lie low, you say," Spence scoffed, his eyes flashing. "We can't just hide forever. We need a plan. A real plan."

As the outlaws galloped into the night, a distant howl of a lone coyote seemed to echo their predicament.

Carter couldn't shake the guilt clawing at him. "Riley, maybe we should give the money back."

Baker's grip on the reins tightened as the muscles in his jaw flexed. "Ain't no turnin' back now, Muley. We're in this deep, and there's no handin' ourselves over to the hangman."

THE THREE OUTLAWS neared a cluster of twisted juniper trees in the shadow of Buzzard Mountain. Baker reined in his horse, his eyes scanning the landscape.

"This is it," Riley said. "We hole up here for the night. Keep watch, and we rotate every couple of hours. We ain't lettin' our guard down for a second."

The outlaws dismounted and silently began to make camp. Carter finally broke the silence.

"Well, tell us Riley, how do we get out of this mess?"

"First we wait. Then we figure out what to do. Ain't no way we're hangin', not if I got any say in it. If Spence hadn't been so quick on the trigger, maybe we wouldn't be in this much trouble."

Spence chimed in. "You said that stagecoach would be loaded, Riley. Loaded with hard cash! All we got was peanuts."

Baker spat onto the ground. "Maybe if you hadn't been so damned eager to shoot, we coulda talked to the driver and guard. Maybe they would've said what they was a carryin'."

Spence's eyes narrowed and he gripped the handle of his pistol. "We had to make a statement. Show 'em we ain't to be messed with."

"Yeah? Well that statement of yours just might get us hung," Baker said.

"You, maybe. But I ain't plannin' on hangin'," Carter said.

Spence shook his head, his voice tinged with frustration. "We're running out of time, and we got four hundred damn dollars to show for it. Baker, you better get us out of this."

Baker's gaze darted between the trees, his mind working. "Like I said, we have to lay low for a while. If the law ain't out after us, a damned bounty hunter will be comin' for sure. But we three stick together no matter what. No point in us fightin' each other."

SOME SEVENTY MILES east of where the three outlaws were, the sun was setting, casting long shadows across the dusty streets of Eastland, Texas. Lucas Cain and Deke Pauley were sitting on the worn-out porch in front of the Cactus Saloon, nursing their beers. They were reflecting on the recent showdown where the two of them had united to save the town from Rufe Sawyer and his gang of ten.

Lucas was a civil war veteran, and his face showed the effects of deadly battles fought, and more than a year spent as a prisoner of war in the notorious Confederate prison at Andersonville. His time since the war had exposed him to dangers, and often the need to kill, to prevent being killed. He took a swig from his beer before breaking the silence.

"I've been thinking, Deke. How would you like to team up with me?"

Pauley adjusted his hat before he looked at Lucas.

"Team up with you—what do you mean?"

"Exactly what it sounds like," Lucas said. "We worked well together here in Eastland. We could ride together and share the bounties we collect. What do you think?"

"It's a little different for me," Deke said. "Everybody knows you wear a badge. And I, well, I just wear a gun."

Lucas laughed. "And you handle it right well. I'd be proud to have you as my partner."

"Are we talking about a fifty-fifty partnership?" Pauley asked.

Lucas nodded his head as he extended his hand. "Fifty-fifty. And anytime we decide it's not working, either one of us can walk away. Is it a deal?"

Pauley shook Lucas's hand. "It's a deal."

THE NEXT MORNING as Lucas and Deke saddled their horses, the town of Eastland was just beginning to stir to life.

Lucas squinted into the distance as he looked down the street toward the newspaper office.

"Havin' second thoughts?" Deke asked, following Lucas's gaze.

"About us being partners? No, I think we work well together."

"That's not what I meant and you know it," Deke said. "Do you want to ride by and see if she's at the office?"

Lucas took a deep breath. "No, I told Carolina goodbye already. It was hard, but I know I did the right thing. She doesn't need a man like me—a man who can't settle down."

"You might be sorry," Deke said. "It seems to me like that little girl took a real fancy to you."

"She did, at least, she said she did," Lucas said. He shook his head as he thought of Rosie, his wife who had died in childbirth back in Missouri. It was almost like if he admitted that he could love another woman, it would be a betrayal to her. "Let's ride, partner." He kicked the sides of Charley Two as he started out at a trot.

Deke followed along behind him, knowing that this was the time to be quiet.

After a couple of hours, Deke pulled up beside Lucas.

"Do you have any idea where we're headin'?"

"I saw the sheriff this morning and he mentioned some trouble over in Taylor County near Buffalo Gap. It seems about a week ago a stagecoach was held up and the driver and shotgun guard were killed. Might be somethin' to look into."

Pauley ran his hand over his chin, considering the proposition. "Then, what do you say, we ride on over to Taylor County, and see if the reward's big enough for both of us."

"What do we want to call our partnership?" Lucas asked.

Pauley chuckled. "How 'bout Cain & Pauley. Let's keep it simple."

Lucas laughed heartily. "I like the sound of that. Cain & Pauley it is."

With that settled, the men continued on to Buffalo Gap. The trail was unforgiving, the sun beating down on them as they pushed their horses to cover the distance quickly.

Upon reaching Buffalo Gap, the two men wasted no time in hunting up the sheriff. They found a building with a hand-painted sign saying Office of Sheriff Barney Upton, the sign suggesting that perhaps the office of sheriff was one that was not a long-term position. When Lucas and Deke stepped into the building, they were met by a man whom they took to be the sheriff. He was a small man—no more than five feet, Lucas thought, but he eyed his visitors with suspicion.

"Are you Sheriff Upton?" Lucas asked.

"At least you can read," the man said. "Now, what are you doing here? Not many people come to Buffalo Gap unless they're up to no good."

Lucas exchanged a glance with Deke. "Maybe we've come to the wrong place," Lucas said. "We've come from Eastland where we helped Sheriff Moore take care of Rufe Sawyer and his gang. The sheriff indicated that you had a little trouble over here—the stage robbed and the driver and guard killed."

"That happened."

"Let's go, Lucas," Deke said. "It's obvious Sheriff Upton doesn't need our help."

"Now, just a minute. I didn't say that," the sheriff said. "You didn't even tell me your names. How am I supposed to know who you are? For all I know, you could be friends of them three killers."

"I'm sorry," Lucas said. "I'm Lucas Cain—Marshal Lucas Cain, and this is Deke Pauley."

"I ain't run acrost you, Marshal, but I've heard of Pauley. You're a bounty hunter ain't you?"

"That's how I make my livin'," Deke said.

"Then why'd you come in here together?"

"We've formed a partnership. Cain and Pauley," Lucas said. "And now that you know who we are, could you tell us anything about this stage robbery?"

The sheriff grunted. "Ain't many folks interested in goin' after that gang. There a mean bunch."

"Then, you know who did this?" Lucas asked as he was getting more and more frustrated.

"Riley Baker, Leon Spence, and Muley Carter."

"Do you know for sure they're the ones who did it?" Pauley asked.

"Yeah, one of the passengers was an old lady who runs the Cubby Hole in Canyon Creek. She recognized 'em, because they ate at her place a couple of times, and run out on her," the sheriff said. "They kilt two men for only four hundred dollars. Such a shame." He began shuffling through some papers on his desk. "I guess this is what you're wantin' to see. They got four hunnert and now the reward's five hunnert apiece. Smith and Ledbetter don't take kindly to their stages being robbed and their people gettin' kilt."

Pauley smiled as he took the paper. "Divided, that's seven hundred 'n fifty dollars, damn near twice what the three of 'em got, and they're goin' to have to split it."

"Yeah," Lucas said. "Mr. Baker, Mr. Spence, and Mr. Carter don't know what's coming."

Pauley nodded in agreement. "I suspect they headed for the hills, thinking they'll be getting away."

"What they don't know is that the formidable team of Cain and Pauley are hot on their trail," Lucas said.

"Formable team of Cain and Pauley," Pauley said with a little laugh. "Yeah, I like that."

The sheriff regarded them for a moment before nodding slowly. "Good luck to you two. I guess if anybody can bring 'em in, it would be a pair like you. God only knows, I can't get up anybody in Buffalo Gap who'd go after 'em."

THE TWO MEN pooled their resources and knowledge. Lucas, with his shooting skills and knowledge of the terrain, was complemented by Pauley's ability to track and shoot as well. As Lucas had said, together they made a formidable team.

The chase led them through rugged landscapes, where the scorching Texas sun beat down on their backs. Lucas and Pauley tracked the outlaws' movements, relying on information from informants and piecing together the puzzle of the robbery.

Pauley scanned the horizon. "You reckon they know we're after 'em?"

Lucas shrugged, his gaze fixed on the trail. "Hard to say, but when they find out who's after 'em, they'll wish they'd never crossed that line."

THE NIGHT HUNG over the rugged terrain like a shroud, concealing the outlaws as they rode through the thickets and rocks. Baker, Spence, and Carter moved swiftly, the only sounds being the plodding of horses' hooves underfoot that were augmented by the distant howls of coyotes.

Not far behind the trio, Lucas and Deke navigated the trail, guided only by the faint glow of the moon filtering through the cloud cover. The air was thick with tension, the howls of coyotes and the distant hoots of owls the only sounds disturbing the eerie silence.

As the two moved cautiously through the shadows, a sudden hail of bullets erupted from the underbrush, catching them off guard. The crackling gunfire echoed through the night, as the outlaws had orchestrated a perfect ambush. Lucas and Deke dove for cover behind some rocks, their senses heightened as adrenaline surged.

Bullets whizzed past, narrowly missing the two men as they returned fire, trying to pinpoint the outlaws' location. The darkness worked against them, and the outlaws seemed to melt into the night.

Deke gritted his teeth, a bead of sweat trickling down his forehead as he exchanged gunfire with the unseen assailants.

Amid the chaos, Lucas felt a searing pain in his shoulder as a bullet grazed him. He winced but pressed on. The outlaws, confident in their surprise attack, continued to fire upon their unknown trackers.

"Head for the rock," Lucas said as quietly as possible. With that, they made a daring dash for cover, zigzagging through the rocks to evade the onslaught. Shards of broken stone crunched beneath their boots as they moved through the maze of rocks, the sound giving proof of their movement. Bullets whistled past, some grazing dangerously close, but they managed to break away from the ambush.

Breathing heavily, Lucas and Pauley joined up behind a large rock formation.

"Did you get hit?" Lucas asked.

"No, how about you?" Deke answered.

"My arm was grazed and it hurts like hell," Lucas said, "but all in all with that many bullets raining down on us, it could have been a lot worse." He tore a strip of fabric from the tail of his shirt and hastily fashioned a makeshift bandage for his arm.

AS THE FIRST light of dawn broke through the clouds, Deke and Lucas exchanged determined glances. The outlaws may have caught them off guard last night, but they weren't about to let their prey slip away. With determination, the two resumed their pursuit through the rugged terrain. They knew the hunt was far from over.

"The sneaky bastards," Deke muttered. "I never dreamed they'd try to take us in the middle of the night. If the moon had been bright, they'd have picked us off for sure."

Lucas nodded. "They won't catch us off guard again. We're close, I can feel it."

As they approached a narrow canyon, Lucas raised his hand, signaling for Deke to pull up.

"There," Lucas whispered, his gaze fixed on a distant ridge. "I saw movement. Get ready."

Deke crouched low. "You think it's them?"

Lucas nodded, his fingers instinctively reaching for the grip of his revolver. "Only one way to find out."

Silently, the two men advanced to where they had seen the movement, their boots crunching on the rocky ground. The canyon walls were on either side of them, creating a natural corridor that amplified the slightest noise.

As they rounded a bend, the outlaws came into view. Riley Baker, Leon Spence, and Muley Carter, unaware that their ambush had failed, were gathered around a small campfire.

Lucas and Deke exchanged a glance, then moved quickly. With a sudden burst of action, they emerged from the canyon, with their guns drawn.

"You boys go ahead and enjoy what's left of your breakfast, then you'll be coming with us," Lucas said, his voice carrying a weight of authority.

The outlaws, caught off guard mid-bite, froze with a mixture of surprise and fear. Muley Carter dropped his biscuit, and Leon Spence choked on a mouthful of coffee. Riley Baker, perhaps the quickest to recover, shot a wary glance at Cain and Pauley.

"What the hell!" Carter blurted out. "Where did you come from?"

"Did you think you left us behind last night?" Deke asked. "Because now you'll be comin' with us. We're taking you in."

"The hell you are!" Spence shouted, his hand jerking to his pistol. Despite Spence's quick draw, Lucas was faster, and a single shot rang out, leaving Spence with a bullet hole in his chest. He collapsed to the ground without uttering a word.

"Don't shoot, don't shoot!" Baker pleaded, throwing his hands in the air.

"Riley, what'd you give up for? We're goin' to hang, sure as shootin'," Carter said.

"They ain't gonna hang us," Baker said. "It was Spence what done the shootin'."

"You men are under arrest," Lucas said as he moved toward them.

"What do you mean, under arrest?" Baker asked. "Ain't you a bounty hunter? You can't arrest people."

"US Marshals can," Lucas said as he revealed the badge on his chest.

"You're a US Marshal? I thought you was a bounty hunter," Carter said.

"I'm both," Lucas clarified with a steely gaze.

"Huh, uh. How can you collect reward money if you're a US Marshal," Baker questioned.

"Let's just say I have an arrangement," Lucas replied. "Now, throw your friend belly down over his horse."

Baker and Carter got Spence onto his horse, just as Lucas had asked. Then Lucas handcuffed both of them.

As the outlaws were secured, Lucas and Deke led them back toward the direction they had come from. The rugged terrain seemed to have lost its earlier charm for the outlaws, now offering a harsh reminder of their failed ambush. With the outlaws on horseback, their hands bound, Lucas and Deke rode beside them. The Texas sun bore down on the small procession, as they made the slow trip back to Buffalo Gap.

"Should've never gone along with this," Muley Carter muttered to himself.

Baker, riding beside him, shot a quick glance at Carter. "Ain't no use cryin' over spilt milk, Muley. We're in it now, and we gotta find a way out."

Deke, riding slightly ahead with Lucas, couldn't help

but overhear their conversation. He turned to Lucas with a sly grin. "You reckon they'll start singin' like canaries once we get 'em locked up?"

Lucas nodded. "They might. But that won't be our problem. It's up to Sheriff Upton now."

Deke laughed. "I wonder if that old coot will be glad to see us this time."

"I expect he will be a little more friendly," Lucas said.

When he could see the town in the distance, Lucas couldn't help but feel a sense of satisfaction. It had been a longer chase than they had expected, but Cain and Pauley had prevailed. The outlaws would face justice for their crimes, and the reward money would soon be theirs.

Sheriff Upton greeted them with a mix of surprise as they rode into town, their captives in tow.

"It's been a while," the sheriff said. "I figured you give up on findin' these hoodlums. Which one is the dead one?"

"Leon Spence," Lucas said. "If it makes any difference, these two say he did the killing of the guard and the driver."

"Don't make a dime's worth of difference," Sheriff Upton said. "Come on, you two. Let's get you back to my hotel."

He waited while Lucas and Deke took Baker and Carter back to the jail cell. Then the sheriff locked them in. "I suspect these two will have a nice speedy trial. The judge should be by this way in a week or so, but you two are lucky. I already sent word to Smith and Ledbetter that you were going after the outlaws. Somebody must've knowed about you boys, 'cause your reward money's here already."

The sheriff walked back to his desk, unlocked the

bottom drawer and took out a box. He withdrew fifteen one-hundred-dollar bills and put them on the desk. "I don't know how you're gonna divide this, but I guess that's up to you."

Lucas picked up seven hundred dollars. "The extra hundred is yours, Deke, but I expect you to pay for a shave and hot bath, a good steak dinner, a room, and of course a couple of beers. When you've done all that, we'll divide up the change."

"That works for me, partner," Deke said.

2

Two days later, Lucas and Deke stopped by the sheriff's office, where they found Sheriff Upton sitting behind his desk, a worn wooden surface cluttered with wanted posters and scattered documents. The sun's rays filtered through the dusty windows, casting a warm glow on the scene.

"Howdy, fellas, are you two hangin' around for the trial?" Sheriff Upton asked. "The judge'll be here the end of this week."

"No, I think you'll be able to handle Baker and Carter without us," Lucas said. "We just came by to say goodbye." Lucas extended his hand. "It's been a pleasure doing business with you, Sheriff."

The sheriff shook hands. "I have to say, I was sort of doubtful when you come a ridin' in here, but you done these parts a favor when you brought them two in. Where you off to now?"

"We're not sure," Deke said. "Do you know of anything else that's happened around here?"

"Funny you should ask," the sheriff said as he rustled through the papers on his desk. "Got word about four more outlaws that they say are meaner than rattlesnakes on a hot day. If you're interested, I'll see what I can find out about 'em."

"Oh, we're interested all right," Lucas said.

"Then I'll see you boys tomorrow."

"What do you say we go down to the saloon and have a quiet celebration?" Pauley suggested. "I'll buy you a beer, and you can buy me a whiskey."

Lucas chuckled. "I'd rather buy a drink for a pretty girl, but you'll do in a pinch."

A few minutes later, the two men stepped into the Mule Skinner Saloon, the swinging doors creaking behind them as they entered. The atmosphere of the establishment enveloped them, with the low hum of conversation, the clinking of glasses, and the discordant notes of an out of tune honky-tonk piano.

Nearly everyone knew that Deke and Lucas were the ones who had brought in Carter and Baker, and they also knew that the pair had just been paid a substantial bounty. As they made their way to the bar, the patrons took notice, and a mix of reactions filled the room.

Most of the saloon's occupants, grateful for the removal of the criminals, offered nods of approval and raised their glasses in a silent toast. The atmosphere seemed to lighten with a sense of relief, and a few patrons even congratulated Cain and Pauley on a job well done.

However, not everyone shared in the celebration. A couple of resentful faces in the corner of the room eyed Lucas and Deke with a mixture of disdain and hostility. They may have had some connection to the captured criminals or more than likely, they disagreed with the whole concept of bounty hunting altogether. The tension between the celebratory mood and the undercurrent of resentment added to the atmosphere.

Ignoring the icy stares from the resentful, Lucas and Deke ordered a round of drinks for everyone. The clinking of glasses and the lively chatter started up again, creating a contrast between the gratitude of the majority and the apparent animosity of a small faction in the saloon.

THE NEXT DAY Lucas and Deke stopped by to talk to the sheriff to see if he had found out any more about the four fugitives he had mentioned.

When they stepped in, Sheriff Upton nodded his greeting toward the two. "I told you I'd get some information for you, and I have. I can tell you, it ain't gonna be easy. Any two of 'em is apt to be a challenge, and there's four of 'em. No, siree. Like I said, it ain't gonna be a walk in the park. Maybe I should try to put a posse together to go out with ya."

Lucas chuckled. "Pauley here is my backup, and I'm his. That about all we need."

"All right, but like I said, there's four of 'em," Sheriff Upton said as he began shuffling through the wanted posters scattered across his desk. He pulled out four and laid them in front of the bounty hunters. "Abe Steward, Cy Mathis, Vern Morris, and Pete Slidell. According to these dodgers, these four have been wreckin' towns from all the way from here to the New Mexico border. Maybe even farther."

Lucas leaned forward, studying the faces on the posters. Each man had a look that spoke of a life spent on the wrong side of the law.

"Abe Steward, he's wanted for rustlin' cattle and shootin' up the Smith place down in Pecan Valley. Mean son of a gun, used to be a hired hand 'round these parts before he turned renegade."

Sheriff Upton pointed at the second poster. "Cy Mathis is a card sharp and a swindler. He cheated the mayor out of his life savings in a poker game over in Rock Ridge. Mayor's been raisin' hell ever since."

Pauley nodded, his eyes fixed on the third poster. "I've heard of this guy—Vern Morris."

"That's him. The varmint's a train robber. Hit the express bound for Austin last week. Killed the messenger and as it turned out, didn't get a thing for it."

Sheriff Upton leaned back in his chair, a grim expression on his face. "And finally, Pete Slidell. Wanted for arson and murder up in Blackwood. Burned down the saloon with the owner still inside."

"Which one of them do you want us to go after first?" Lucas asked.

"It doesn't matter who's first, since the four of 'em formed a gang, and they're all together now. They robbed a bank over in Coyote Creek last week."

"How much money did they get away with?" Pauley asked.

"Thirty-five hundred dollars." The sheriff chuckled. "Funny thing is that amount's equal to what you fellas'll get if you bring 'em all in."

Lucas tapped his fingers on the worn wooden table. "Are these dead or alive warrants?"

"It don't say, so I'd guess they want 'em alive preferably, but it don't say anybody'd shed any tears if it comes out the other way."

Sheriff Upton handed the wanted posters to Lucas and Pauley. "Good luck, boys. And don't let these hombres give you too much trouble. You can guess the bounty on their heads is set high for a reason."

LUCAS AND DEKE rode out of Buffalo Gap, their horses kicking up trails of dust in their wake. The quiet little town faded into the distance as they headed toward Coyote Creek where the bank robbery had occurred.

Lucas and Deke had been on the trail of the four men for the better part of a week, and up until now they had not found them. It might be more accurate to say that the outlaws had found them, because as they approached an old, abandoned building, they came under fire. The four men they were trailing had taken refuge in the loft of the barn.

Both Lucas and Deke leaped down from their horses then sent them out of the line of fire. The two dived for the ground and took what cover they could behind the bottom plank of what was left of the old corral fence.

A few bullets slapped into the plank, while others snapped by overhead.

"Deke," Lucas called over to him.

When Deke looked over, Lucas held up four fingers, then pointed to the barn. Deke nodded that he understood, then raised up to take a look. Instantly, one of the outlaws took advantage of his exposure and took a shot. The bullet hit the narrow fence post behind which Deke had taken cover, sending splinters into his face, then passing on with a careening whine. It was the closest any of the bullets had gotten to either of them so far.

"You all right?" Lucas called.

"Yeah, I should have had more sense than to raise my head," Deke replied.

Earlier that morning, the four outlaws had killed a rancher, Karl Schafer, stealing the seventeen hundred and fifty dollars he had been paid for the cattle he had just sold. They thought they had gotten away with it, but a neighboring rancher was on his way over to see Schafer, and he had seen the whole thing.

"Deke," Lucas called out.

When Deke turned toward him, Lucas let it be known with words and gestures that he was going to go wide, then approach the barn from the left and that Deke should do so from the right.

Before they left their positions, both fired a couple shots at the four men. Then, as the shooting was returned, Lucas and Deke bent over to lower their profile and started toward the left and right sides of the barn.

"Where the hell are they?" Mathis asked.

"Right behind you," Lucas called, stepping out from the corner. "Drop your guns."

"Shoot 'em, shoot 'em!" Steward shouted, and he turned to shoot at Lucas. The four outlaws began shooting and Lucas and Deke returned fire. The four outlaws missed, Lucas and Deke didn't. All four outlaws tumbled forward, falling from the loft. Only Steward was still alive and he was drawing labored breaths, indicating that he wouldn't be alive but for a few more minutes.

"Who the hell are you?" Steward asked around gasping breaths.

"I'm Lucas Cain, he's Deke Pauley."

"It's nice meeting you," Pauley said with a mocking smile.

"Son of a bitch. I shoulda known." Steward drew his last breath.

Lucas gave a whistle, and Charley Two, his horse, came trotting up to him. Pauley's horse came up as well.

"Glad you've got Charley Two trained. He not only comes to you when you whistle, he brings Dodger with him."

It was mid-afternoon when Lucas and Deke rode back into Buffalo Gap, each of them leading two horses, with the bodies of the outlaws draped over the saddles.

"That's Lucas Cain," someone said in awe.

"Yeah, 'n the other's Deke Pauley," a second man added. "They was just here a while back. You 'member, they brought in Riley Baker and his bunch. Course Leon Spence was already dead."

"Them was the ones that got hung, warn't they? I wasn't here to see it, but I heard about it."

"Cain 'n Pauley is about the best bounty hunters in the whole state," another said.

"Yeah, if you ever get the law after you, you sure as hell don't want them two comin' for you."

"Oh, that's right—Cain is the law."

Lucas and Deke dismounted in front of Sheriff Upton's office, tied off the six horses, then went inside.

"Don't tell me you got 'em already?" the sheriff asked.

"We've got all four of 'em outside," Lucas said. "We'd like to collect the bounties and then get underway."

"You've got them outside?" the sheriff replied. "Good Lord, man, what if they run off?"

Pauley laughed. "That's not likely to happen. They're belly down."

"I see. Do you know for sure who they are?"

"Abe Steward, Cy Mathis, Vern Morris, and Pete Slidell," Lucas said. "Just like you sent us after."

"Good. And belly down is the best way to bring those sons of bitches in," the sheriff replied. "Don't have to get the judge or pay the hangman."

"Where do you want to eat?" Lucas asked as he and Deke left the sheriff's office. "I'm a little tired of trail food."

"What about there?" Deke replied, pointing toward a building with a sign that read, Table and Plate. "Seems to me like that's a place we could get us some fine vittles."

"All right," Lucas answered.

Going inside they found an empty table and were met by a boy of about fifteen or so. "What'll you have?" the boy asked.

"What's good here?" Lucas replied.

"Anything my mama cooks is good," the boy answered.

"That's good enough for us," Deke said.

The two ordered steak and eggs, and their order was quickly delivered.

"This is a hell of a lot better 'n what we've been eatin'," Lucas said as he cut into his steak.

"What? Are you telling me you don't like my cooking?" Deke asked, a smile crossing his face. "I think I do a damn fine job with beans and bacon."

"I agree, but we both should be good at it, 'cause we've sure as hell cooked enough of' em over the years."

The two men enjoyed their meal and for the next few minutes the only sound was that of the utensils hitting the plates. Deke broke the silence.

"Do you still think about her?"

"Think about who?"

Pauley made a sound that might have been a laugh.

"You know damn well who I'm talking about."

"Yeah, I do," Lucas said. "I might have to find my way back to Eastland to check in on Miss Carolina McKay."

"Lucas, I have to say that I'm surprised you left town when you did. If someone that pretty said the things you said she said to you, I think I would have pulled up under her table anytime she asked me to," Deke said. "Why, I would have put my guns away, too. All for the love of a good, decent woman."

"I have to admit that telling Carolina goodbye was one of the hardest things I've ever had to do, but I know she'd expect me to take over her father's newspaper someday. She's so dedicated to it, and she's good at what she does, but there is...I don't know, I just can't see myself writin' news stories, or worse yet, trying to sell ads to keep that newspaper goin'."

"I guess I can understand that. She sure is a pretty thing though," Deke said.

"Yeah? Well you just keep your hands off my woman," Lucas said with a little chuckle.

"You don't have to worry about that. Her heart's so set on you, that in her eyes, nobody else even exists."

The smile left Lucas's face. "I know that. But, hard as

it was to leave her, I know in the long run I did her a favor. I could never be the man she really wanted."

As Lucas and Deke ate their supper, they discussed what they should do next, but didn't come up with any solid plan. But as it so happened, events were taking place a hundred miles southwest of Buffalo Gap which would soon get their attention.

3

In the town of Comanche Springs, four men dismounted in front of the town cafe, then went inside and ordered ham, eggs, biscuits, and fried potatoes. Their food came, and to anyone watching who had not seen their faces on wanted posters, they appeared merely to be four friends lingering over a meal for some friendly conversation.

Shortly after ten o'clock, the four men left the restaurant. Ike Sanford rode to the north end of town, Logan Murphy went to the south, while Clem Anders and Wilson Puckett casually walked their horses across the street and hitched them directly in front of the bank. For a few minutes they stood at the door, then Sandford came galloping into town from the north end of the street while Murphy came riding from the other end at a full gallop. Both men were shooting into the air and whooping loudly, scattering the terrified bystanders. With the citizens' attention diverted from the bank, Clem Anders and Wilson Puckett rushed inside.

"Put your hands up!" Anders shouted gruffly the moment they stepped through the door.

The two women customers screamed, while one male customer shouted out in anger, only to be clubbed down by the butt of Puckett's pistol.

"Ever'one keep quiet," Anders shouted. "We'll do all the talkin'." He pointed his pistol at the teller and handed him two cloth bags.

"You, take these and empty them drawers. And be quick about it."

With shaking hands, the teller began scooping money out of the open drawers and dropping it into the two bags.

"Now let's get to the real money. You," Puckett said to the bank teller who was standing nearest the vault. "Start emptyin' out that safe."

The middle-aged banker put his hand on the door, then to Puckett's surprise, he abruptly slammed it shut.

"That was a stupid thing to do. You're just gonna have to open it up again," Puckett said.

With a smug smile, the banker shook his head. "Not 'til eight o'clock tomorrow morning, I won't be opening it."

"What do you mean?"

"It's a time-lock. It's impossible for anyone to open it before eight tomorrow. So, you're just going to have to find another bank to rob."

"Damn you!" Puckett shouted. Without a moment's hesitation, he shot the banker in the chest.

Eyes growing wide, the banker gasped, fell against the front of the vault, then slid down to a sitting position, leaving on the vault door, a swath of blood from his exit wound. He took two or three gasping breaths, then died.

"The cash drawers empty?" Puckett asked.

"Yes," Anders answered.

"Then let's get the hell out of here."

The bank president, unnoticed by Anders and Puckett, was in the back room. When the robbery started, he sneaked out the back door. Once clear of the bank, he darted up between two buildings until he was in the middle of Main Street. There, he began shouting, "The bank is being robbed! The bank is being robbed!"

The townspeople suddenly recognized the great show of gunplay for the ruse it was and began arming themselves. Ducking behind barrels and crates, the men started firing at the mounted outlaws. The outlaws quit firing in the air and began shooting back.

Logan Murphy shot one man as he rose up from behind a crate to get off a shot from his rifle. The man gasped in pain, then fell.

The outlaws jerked their horses about, making them prance so as to be more difficult targets. They waited anxiously for their cohorts to emerge from the bank, firing off shot after shot as they kept the townspeople busy.

Inside the bank, the customer that Anders had clubbed to the floor, regained consciousness. Seeing what was going on, he managed to pull his gun.

"Hold it right there!" he shouted.

Anders turned toward the customer and fired. He missed. The customer fired back and didn't miss. Anders put his hands over his stomach wound, then went down.

"You son of a bitch!" Puckett shouted. He shot the customer in the chest, then he rushed out the front door of the bank holding the money sacks with the bills taken from the cash drawers. Most of the bank's money was left behind, untouched, on the shelves of the time-lock vault. When Puckett stepped out of the bank, he was stopped in his tracks by the sight of the battle taking place just down the street.

He wondered what was going on. It looked as if they were engaged in a full-scale war!

Seeing Puckett come out of the bank, two of the closest citizens of the town turned toward him.

"Hold it! You ain't goin' nowhere!" a middle-aged townsman called. At almost the same time he yelled, he fired his pistol. The bullet missed Puckett and punched through the front window of the bank. Another man fired a shot and his bullet went through Puckett's hat.

"Let's go, let's go!" Ike Sanford yelled to the others.

"Where's Clem?" Logan Murphy shouted.

"He's dead. Let's go!"

From the restaurant in which the men had eaten a few minutes earlier, a citizen, food stains spattered on the front of his shirt, appeared with a shotgun. He let go a blast, but the gun was loaded with a light bird shot, and his pellets merely peppered the outlaws without penetrating their skin. Another man with a shotgun fired, and the second bank window came crashing down.

With the three remaining outlaws mounted, they galloped toward the south end of town. Seeing them come that way, some men rolled a wagon out into the middle of the dusty street and tipped it over, creating a barricade. Several of the townsmen gathered around the wagon then, with rifles held at the ready.

"What the hell? What do we do now, Puckett?" Sanford asked.

"This way!" Puckett shouted back, and he reined his mount around, turning toward the large plate-glass window fronting a dressmaking shop. He urged the horse forward, and the animal leaped through the window, shattering the glass with an enormous crashing sound, and clearing the way for the other horses that followed close behind.

There were several women in the shop, including one who was being fitted for a new dress. Covering her half-naked, corseted body with her arms, she and the other ladies screamed in terror as they made a mad dash to get out of the way. The horses clattered and skidded across the wooden floor, then ran through the back door and into an open field behind the store. It was a brilliant move on the part of the outlaws, for none of the townspeople were yet mounted, and by the time they managed to reach their horses and come around the edge of town, the bank robbers had completely disappeared into the hills.

The stunned citizens of the town began to count the dead. There were three in the bank, Manny Clark, the brave teller who had slammed the door shut on the vault, J. T. Bentley, the customer who had attempted to stop the robbers, and one of the outlaws. Out in the street, three men and a young boy had been killed. The deputy sheriff was among those killed.

TOTALLY UNAWARE OF the bank robbery and murder in Pecos County, Lucas and Deke had collected the bounty due them and continued their ride which, by now, had taken them into West Texas. They were in Reeves County, and as they crested a small hill, they looked out over the open, semi-arid land that lay before them. It had been almost three months since they had left Eastland.

They had no specific destination in mind, but they

knew they were somewhere in West Texas. Lucas held his hand up as a signal to Deke.

"Let's stop here for a little while. We need to give our horses a break," Lucas said, as he wiped the sweat from his face.

"All right, then we might as well have somethin' to eat ourselves," Deke said.

"Sounds good. I'll have chicken 'n dumplins', dressing, some corn, biscuit, and a glass of beer," Lucas said.

"Blueberry, or cherry pie for dessert?" Deke asked.

"Uhhm, I'd say apple."

"I'm sorry, we don't have any apple pie."

"Oh, well, then just forget it, if you don't have any apple pie, I'll just have a piece of jerky and some beans," Lucas said.

Pauley laughed. "Lucas, you say the damndest things."

"How far do you reckon it is to the next town?" Lucas asked.

"I was out in this part of the state about a year or two ago," Deke answered as he looked around to get a feel for the lay of the land. "If I remember right, we ought to be coming into San Martin before nightfall."

Lucas grinned. "Well, then, a steak and a beer for supper may be in the picture after all."

Stopping, they found a couple of rocks to sit on while they shared a can of beans and a couple strips of jerky. The two partners finished their lunch, then remounted to continue their ride.

They were much closer than Pauley realized, because they rode into town no more than an hour later. Even though Lucas had never been to San Martin before, there was a familiarity to it, because it was like so many other towns Lucas had visited. The street was wide enough to allow two wagons to meet, and lined on both sides with stores, shops, offices, and houses. Two of the businesses were saloons, so they stopped at the first one. The sign out front identified the saloon as Nippy Jones Tavern.

Because it was mid-afternoon, there weren't many customers. Two men stood at the other end of the bar, and three were sitting at a table. There were two bar girls sitting alone at a table in the far corner, and they both got up and with practiced smiles, approached Lucas and Deke.

"Well, I haven't seen either one of you two handsome gentlemen before," one of the girls said.

"Did you hear that, Deke?" Lucas asked. "Here we bought these two beautiful young ladies half a dozen drinks just last week, and now they say they don't even remember us."

"What?" one of the girls asked with a shocked expression on her face. "What night was that?"

"Never mind. If you two can't remember us, I suppose we didn't make that much of an impression on you. What do you say, Deke, should we buy them a few more drinks and see if they remember us this time?"

"We might as well," Deke said with a little chuckle.

Lucas and Deke each got a beer, and the girls got a small shot glass drink each, then the four of them found a table.

"So, what's interesting in the town of San Martin?" Lucas asked.

"Why, we're interesting, honey. My name is Annie, and her name is Suzie."

Lucas and Deke talked with the two bar girls for a while, and even as they were talking to Annie and Suzie, Lucas's thoughts drifted back to Carolina. Would it always be like this? Every woman he met would remind him of Carolina?

"Lucas?" Deke asked as he poked his friend in the ribs.

"What?"

"Where were you just now? I asked if you wanted to go have supper."

Lucas looked at Deke and the two bar girls who were sharing their table. He wasn't in Eastland, and he wasn't talking to Carolina.

"Oh, uh, yes, let's do go to supper, but first, I think we should stop by the sheriff's office."

When Lucas and Deke went into the sheriff's office a few minutes later, they saw two men playing checkers.

"Are one of you the sheriff?" Lucas asked.

"He is," one of the two men said, pointing to the man across the checkerboard from him. "But after I beat him this time, he's going to resign, then I'll be the sheriff, and he'll be my deputy. Right now I'm Sheriff Mason's deputy, Ken Watson."

"Damn, I had no idea it worked like that," Sheriff Mason said as he jumped three crowned checkers in one move. He looked up toward Lucas and Deke. "What can I do for you two?"

"I'm Lucas Cain, this is Deke Pauley, we'd..."

"Like to see my reward posters," Mason said.

"Yeah, how'd you know that?" Deke asked.

"Well, when two well-known bounty hunters show up in a sheriff's office, it's either to cash in a couple of outlaws, or to look at the reward posters, and I don't see any bodies draped over your horses."

"Damn, that's pretty good reasoning, you ought to go into law work," Lucas said with a smile.

"Ike Sanford, Logan Murphy, and Wilson Puckett. There's a thousand dollars on each of 'em," Sheriff Mason said.

"A thousand dollars on each of 'em?" Deke asked, his eyes opening wide.

"What did they do?" Lucas asked.

"They robbed a bank, and killed half a dozen people down in Comanche Springs."

"What do you think, Deke?" Lucas asked.

"Fifteen hundred dollars each? Hell yeah," Deke said.

4

As Ike Sanford, Logan Murphy, and Wilson Puckett rode through the open range, dust billowed behind them. They had been on the run for the better part of a week, and now found themselves deep in the wilderness, seeking any place of refuge in the open range. The stolen money was in their saddlebags, a heavy reminder of the blood-stained path they now tread.

Under the cover of darkness, they set up camp in a secluded canyon, surrounded by cliffs that shielded them from prying eyes. The crackling campfire cast shadows on their faces as they huddled together to discuss their next move.

Ike, the self-appointed leader, spoke in a low, gravelly voice, "We can't stay out here forever. We have to find us someplace to be."

Logan nodded in agreement. "We need to get out of Texas—maybe head for the border."

Wilson, the quiet member of the trio, made no observation, and by his silence agreed to go along with whatever the other two decided.

The moon hung high in the sky as they packed up their makeshift camp. Silently, they rode through the night, guided only by the stars. They stuck to the less-traveled trails, avoiding any signs of civilization that might expose them.

As dawn broke, they found themselves in a ghost town, its dilapidated buildings bearing witness to a bygone era. The wind whispered through the deserted streets. The trio decided to rest for the day, taking refuge in the crumbling remains of an abandoned saloon.

Time passed slowly as they lay low, nursing their anxieties. If any distant sound reached their ears, paranoia set in. Every creak of the abandoned building seemed to signal an approaching threat.

The sun dipped below the horizon once again, casting the ghost town in eerie shadows. Under the cover of darkness, the three men mounted their horses once more, continuing their desperate journey. They rode on, each one haunted by the echoes of what they had done.

The three outlaws chose a place where they were sure they would be safe for the night. But they miscalculated, because on their eighth night on the run, Lucas and Deke saw the glow of a campfire and cautiously approached. Thinking it might be some cowboys in the middle of a roundup, bedded down for the night, they moved close enough to be able to see and hear what was going on. They weren't too surprised to discover that it wasn't cowboys at all. From the overheard conversation, they learned that it was the three men they were looking for. They were discussing the bank robbery in Comanche Springs.

"Eleven hunnert dollars," one of them said. "We hit a bank, we been on the run for the better part of a week, and all the hell we got to show for it is eleven hunnert dollars. Just what the hell did you and Anders do in there?" one of the men asked.

"I told you, the son of a bitch closed the door to the vault, and it couldn't be opened until the next day. I shot 'im."

Deke and Lucas moved a little closer for a better look and to hear more of what the three men were discussing. As they did so, Pauley's foot dislodged a large rock, and it tumbled down, noisily.

"What the hell was that?" Sanford yelled, his pan of beans flying as he stood up quickly, his gun in his hand in an instant. "Puckett, douse them flames," he ordered. Coffee was immediately thrown on the fire, and it sizzled and smoked as it went out.

Fearing discovery, Lucas and Deke started to scramble over the rocky ground to get away.

"There! I saw something!" one of the outlaws shouted, and the shout was followed almost immediately by a shot.

The others began to fire as well, and as they fired the flames from the muzzles of their guns lit up the dark like flashes of lightning. A bullet passed so close to his ear that Lucas could feel the puff of air at its passing.

Using the muzzle flashes as targets, Lucas returned fire. He heard a yelp of pain.

"After him!" one of the bandits shouted. "The son of a bitch hit Murphy!"

Another shot was fired, and it hit a rock by Pauley's feet, digging out a piece of the rock and slamming it painfully into his leg. He was thankful for the thick, sturdy denim cloth that protected the skin; otherwise, the shard would have penetrated as if it were a slug.

Intuitively, Deke zigged to one side, just as the ground where he had been was struck by a bullet, sending a piece of sod into the air.

The outlaws kept up their barrage of shooting as they approached.

Suddenly the ground gave way in front of Deke, and he fell over the edge of the cliff. Involuntarily, he let out a yell as he fell.

"We got him!" someone yelled.

"We didn't get him, he fell over the damn cliff."

"Who was he? Did you see him, Puckett?" Sanford asked.

"No, it was too dark, I don't have no idea who he is."

"You mean who he was," Sanford said. "More 'n likely he's dead now."

"Wonder if he was the only one?" Puckett said.

"I want to see his body," Sanford said.

"And just how are you gonna do that? He's at the bottom of the cliff, three or four hundred feet down," Puckett said. "He's dead."

"He ain't dead, 'till I see him dead," Sanford said ominously.

"You men drop your guns," Lucas ordered, stepping into the aura of light from the campfire.

"We can see 'im, shoot 'im!" Sanford yelled.

Lucas realized then that he was backlit by the fire, so he jumped out of the glow. Sanford and Puckett both began firing but because Lucas had moved quickly, the three outlaws had no target. Lucas did have a target, and he shot back, aiming at the muzzle flashes. There was a brief exchange of fire, then the shooting stopped.

Lucas stood quietly for a moment, listening. He heard the moans of one of the men, and he approached quietly.

When he reached them, he saw that two were dead, and the other nearly so. He kicked both guns out of the way, then walked over to the edge of the cliff and looked down. He saw that Pauley had managed to grab a small, sideways growing tree to break his fall.

"Hang on, Deke!" Lucas called. "I'm goin' to get you back up here."

"Yeah, well, you better do it in a hurry. I'm gettin' tired of hangin' here." Deke called back.

Lucas ran back to his horse. "I'm goin' to need your help," he said to his horse.

Charley Two whickered and nodded his head as if he understood. Lucas led him back to the edge of the cliff, then took down the rope and quickly formed a noose and slip knot. He tied one end of the rope to the saddle horn, then took the noose to the edge.

"I've got a rope here," he called down to Deke.

"I...I don't know if I can hold on to it," Deke said, the exhaustion showing in his voice.

"You won't need to. All you have to do is get an arm through the loop, and Charley Two will pull you up."

"Drop the rope as soon as you can."

"Here it comes."

Lucas lowered the rope until it reached Deke. He got one arm through the loop, then hanging onto it, got his other arm through. He wanted to get it around his waist, but he knew he couldn't. Where it was would have to do.

"Pull me up," he shouted.

Deke felt the noose growing tighter. It was so tight that it hurt. Then he felt himself being pulled up over the edge. Once he was safely recovered, Lucas removed the noose, and Deke lay there, fighting to recover his breath.

Deke started to get to his feet, but as he stood, he

collapsed in pain. When Lucas went to him, he saw a protruding bone in his lower leg.

"I'm sorry, partner," Deke said.

The moonlight bathed the scene as Deke lay on the ground, his broken leg causing him immense pain. Lucas stood by, assessing the situation. The three outlaws were either dead or were dying, and their horses were nearby.

Lucas knew he had to get Deke back to San Martin as soon as possible. He looked around, spotting the three lifeless bodies of the outlaws. With a heavy sigh, he made a quick decision.

"Deke," Lucas said, crouching down beside him, "I need to get you back to town. It's the only way to save your leg. I'll come back for the bodies."

"No," Deke said, his face twisted in pain. "Leave me here, but get the bodies back to San Martin." He grimaced as he tried to move his leg. "Three thousand dollars."

"There's no way I'm leaving you," Lucas said as he hurried over to the outlaws' horses, untying them and removing the saddles. He drug the lifeless bodies to a slight elevation, then with the horses as close as possible he manhandled the limp bodies belly down onto the horses. He tied their hands and legs together with a piece of rope he had found attached to one of the saddles. It was a gruesome task, and the moonlight seemed to highlight the stark brutality of their situation.

Once the horses were loaded, Lucas turned his attention to Deke who was now fading in and out of consciousness. He knew they needed to get to San Martin as quickly as possible.

"I'm going to lift you onto my horse, Deke. I know it's going to hurt, but we have to get going."

Deke braced himself, and with Lucas's help, he was

hoisted onto Charley Two, his broken leg carefully positioned to minimize the pain. Lucas tied the three horses carrying the outlaw's bodies to Deke's horse, then fastened a long rope so that he could lead the four horses with a minimum of effort. As gently as possible, Lucas climbed onto Charley Two sitting behind Deke. They began the slow and arduous journey back to San Martin, the night air filled with the sounds of coyotes that seemed to be getting closer. Deke gritted his teeth, enduring the excruciating pain as they rode.

Hours later, they finally reached San Martin, just as the first hints of dawn began coloring the sky. Lucas wasted no time in getting Deke to the doctor's office. As they arrived, he noticed a sign that read "Dr. Hal Simpson, MD."

Dr. Simpson emerged from the office, his eyes widening in surprise at the sight of Deke's condition. "What happened here?" he exclaimed.

Lucas explained the situation, and with the doctor's assistance, they carefully got Deke inside. Dr. Simpson assessed the broken leg, and his expression grew serious. "This is a bad break, but I can set it. It's going to be painful, Deke."

Deke nodded, his face pale with pain but filled with determination. As Dr. Simpson began his work, his daughter, Julia, entered the room to assist.

Lucas watched as Deke gritted his teeth and endured the pain. After the leg was set and Deke was resting, Lucas stepped outside the doctor's office, his heart heavy with the events of the night.

"Will he lose his leg, Doc?" Lucas asked.

"It's hard to tell," Dr. Simpson said. "If we can keep him off it for a while, and if he doesn't get gangrene, the chances are good, but he won't be out on the trail for a long time."

"I understand," Lucas said. He stepped out on the porch, expecting to see the three dead men draped over their horses, just as he had left them, but they were gone.

He immediately headed for Sheriff Mason's office. It would be like someone to turn the bodies in for the reward, especially when it was for three thousand dollars.

"Did you by any chance run across the bodies of Sanford, Murphy, and Puckett?" Lucas asked as he burst into the sheriff's office.

"I got 'em," Sheriff Mason said. "They're down at the undertaker's place right now."

"You know Deke and I brought them in," Lucas said.

"I know," the sheriff said with a chuckle. "Julia Simpson came to tell us what was goin' on as soon as her dad got Pauley into his office. Seems she didn't like the thoughts of havin' 'em hangin' out in front of the doc's office."

Lucas took a deep breath. "It's been quite a long twenty-four hours." He took off his hat and ran his hand through his hair. "You wouldn't happen to have an extra cup of coffee would you?"

"I do. Grab a cup off that shelf and pour yourself a cup. Ain't got no sugar or milk, if that's how you like it."

"Black is fine," Lucas said as he plopped down on a chair in front of the sheriff's desk.

"You look a little tuckered, Cain," Sheriff Mason said. "When was the last time you caught a little shuteye?"

"To tell you the truth, I don't rightly remember."

"I ain't got nobody in jail to be a botherin' you. If you'd like, you can go on back and sleep for a while," the sheriff said.

"That sounds so good," Lucas said, "but I need to see to the horses."

"No need. My deputy took all five of 'em down to the livery. When Ken comes in, I'll send him down to make sure they've been fed."

"Thanks, Sheriff, I'll take you up on your offer," Lucas said as he headed back toward one of the empty cells.

5

The next morning, or what he thought was the next morning, Lucas awakened in the jail cell. For an instant, he couldn't remember why he was here, and then it came to him.

Deke. He had to get to Deke to see how he was doing.

He sat up on the side of the cot as he rubbed his hand over his face. He knew his beard was at least a week old. He needed to find Charley Two and see if his gear was still intact.

"I thought I heard somebody rustlin' around back here," Sheriff Mason said as he came back to the cell. "Some cowboy's mighty glad you was here. I almost threw him in here with you, but then I thought you needed the rest more than the cowboy needed to sleep off his drunk."

"I'm sorry about that," Lucas said as he looked toward the window. "What time is it?"

"Son, it's near 'bout eleven o'clock—eleven o'clock a day and a half later."

"Damn," Lucas said as he rose quickly. "I need to get

out of here. I need to check on Deke. He probably thinks I took the bounty and ran out on him."

"Nah, he knows what's been goin' on. Miss Julia's been runnin' back and forth keepin' me up to date on how Pauley's been fairin'."

"And what is the report?" Lucas asked.

"It's hard to tell," the sheriff said. "It seems he's been sleepin' pert near as long as you have."

"At least he's staying still," Lucas said. "The doctor said that was one of the things he would have to do for a while—if he wants to keep his leg, that is."

The sheriff started to leave the cell area, but then he turned around. "What's next for you two?"

"I don't know," Lucas said. "It sounds like Deke's goin' to be laid up for quite a while."

"If I got my facts right, it seems there was a time you two run your separate ways."

"We did," Lucas said. "It's less than a year that Deke and I have been partners."

"Are you interested in goin' out alone?"

"That depends on who you want tracked down," Lucas said, "and it depends on what happens to Deke."

"I understand, but I've got a couple I'd sure like to see brought to justice," the sheriff said. "There are two of 'em but they don't run together. To be honest with you, I'm not sure they ever even met each other."

"All right, what are their names?" Lucas asked.

"The two men with the highest bounties are John Babcock and Press Gibson, a thousand dollars for each of 'em. But for me, Babcock is the one I'd most like to see brought in. He kilt a preacher, and the widow woman that was workin' as the cleanin' lady, then he stole the money that had been raised to build a new church."

"He sounds like a doozy," Lucas said. "What did Gibson do?"

"He killed a man over a poker game," Sheriff Mason said. "There really wasn't that big of an argument over the card game, it's just that Gibson's fast, very fast, and the way I heard it, he forced the shooting so he could show off."

"Do you have a description of them?" Lucas asked.

"Better'n that, I have an actual photograph of Babcock."

Sheriff Mason opened a drawer on his desk and pulled out a photograph. "This was taken last year when we picked him up for stealin' a couple of calves from Seamus Crowley. 'Course he didn't kill nobody then, and Crowley got his calves back, so Judge Felker didn't send 'im off to prison, he only give him two months here in jail."

"What about Gibson?"

"No picture of him, and since he's not from here, I never seen him. The only description I have of him is that he's short with dark hair and brown eyes. But, if you're goin' after anybody, I wish you'd go after Babcock first. The whole town was pretty upset when Reverend Philpot was took down. He didn't deserve that. A good man," the sheriff said.

"Does Babcock have any friends or relatives here in town?" Lucas asked.

"There's people here in town that know 'im, but there ain't nobody that would claim him as a relative or even a friend."

"Who do you suggest that I see first?" Lucas asked.

"I'd say Wanda Jane Carmichael would be a good place to start. She was Mrs. Stokes' sister. Mary Beth Stokes is the widow woman that Babcock killed."

"Where might I find the Carmichael woman?" Lucas asked.

"You'll find her down at the Threads and Things. That's a store that sells women's dresses, and Mrs. Carmichael does sewin' for Homer Dawson. He owns the place."

"Thank you, Sheriff," Lucas said.

"Cain?" Sheriff Mason called.

Lucas turned to look back toward the sheriff.

"I know you're worried about your partner, but you'd be doin' ever' body in town a favor if you could bring that son of a bitch back, either alive so we can hang 'im, or dead, lyin' belly down across his saddle. It really don't matter which, just so you get him."

WHEN LUCAS ENTERED the Threads and Things, he met the man whom he presumed to be the owner. He was a thin and very neatly dressed man, with a closely cropped mustache.

"Yes, sir, what can I do for you? Are you looking for something for the lady?" he asked.

Lucas held out his marshal's badge. "Mr. Dawson?"

Dawson looked a little nervous. "Yes, I'm Homer Dawson."

"I wonder if you would give Mrs. Carmichael some time to talk to me. It's about her sister," Lucas said.

"Oh, yes, of course, the poor woman who was killed. I know that Wanda Jane has taken that very hard. I'm sure she would like to talk to anyone who would bring the man who killed her sister to justice."

Dawson took Lucas to the back of the shop where he saw someone sitting over a sewing machine, the needle of which was moving up and down, rapidly operated by a foot pedal. Wanda Jane was a small woman with her gray hair tied up in a bun.

"Have you got a moment, Wanda Jane?" Dawson asked.

"I'm letting out a dress for Miss Walsh," Wanda Jane said.

"You can finish it later. Miss Walsh will understand. This man is a US Marshal, and he wants to talk to you about your sister."

"Yes, sir, if it would help you find the...well, I won't use the word I would like to, to describe him. But I'll gladly talk to you."

"Did you or your sister know John Babcock?" Lucas asked.

"That depends on what you mean by knowing him. Babcock didn't go to church, but Mary Beth said that he would sometimes stop by the church beggin' for enough money to buy somethin' to eat."

"And would he get the money?" Lucas asked.

"Oh, yes, Reverend Philpot was a very generous man."

"And this is how Babcock repaid him," Lucas said.

"And my sister," Wanda Jane added.

"Do you know if Babcock had any kind of a job?" Lucas asked.

"I don't know if he had a regular job, but I think Mary Beth told me once, that from time to time he would do a little work for Jeb Turner. Mr. Turner owns the livery."

"Thank you, Mrs. Carmichael. You've been most helpful," Lucas said.

The livery was not far from the Threads and Things, so Lucas walked the short distance. He felt guilty about not stopping at Doctor Simpson's place first, but he decided he needed to get as much information as possible before he spoke with Deke.

"Yes, sir, are you wantin' to take out a horse?" a white-haired, muscular-looking man asked.

"No, I'm Marshal Cain, and I believe you are boarding my horse."

"Is your horse one of the ones Deputy Watson brung in?"

"Yes, that's him in the last stall," Lucas said as he moved toward Charley Two. "How much do I owe you?"

"You don't owe me nothin', Marshal. I know you and your partner brought in them three hoodlums and the whole town's much obliged."

"Well, thank you," Lucas said as he turned away from Charley Two. "If you don't mind, I'd like to ask you some questions."

"About what?"

"It's more about who," Lucas said. "Mrs. Carmichael told me that John Babcock worked for you."

"Yeah, John worked for me from time to time, if you can actually call it work," Turner said. "About half the time I had to go around behind him cleanin' up the mess he caused. On the day he left, he stole a horse from me."

"Oh?"

"Yeah, as it turned out, it was right after he kilt Reverend Philpot and Mrs. Stokes. A grulla it was, finest horse I had. I'll say this for the son of a bitch, he did know his horseflesh."

"Thanks, Mr. Turner, you've been helpful," Lucas said.

"Humph, wish I could tell you which way to head

out," Turner said. "That is, you are goin' to hunt the varmit down, ain't ya?"

Lucas scrunched up his face. "It depends," Lucas said. "I need to talk to my partner."

"Then what you're a tellin' me is, you ain't gonna go. Ever'body in town knows that Pauley fella is in a bad way," Turner said. "If you're a waitin' on him to be up and around, you'll be here 'til Christmas."

Lucas took a deep breath. "I'll be taking Charley Two now, and I thank you for boarding him for me."

Jeb Turner smiled and nodded his head. "Marshal, I think you just made up your mind."

BEFORE GOING BACK to see the sheriff, Lucas headed for the doctor's office.

"Good afternoon, Marshal Cain," Julia Simpson said when he opened the door. "Mr. Pauley has been asking about you."

"That's good. Is he awake?" Lucas asked.

"He is, but be careful, he's in an awful grumpy mood right now," Julia said.

"And why is that?"

"My dad just told him the good and the bad news, and he didn't take it too well."

"Should I know what he said before I head back there?" Lucas asked.

Julia rolled her eyes. "He'll tell you. Go on back."

Lucas went through the hall to the back of the doctor's office. There were two small rooms that were examining rooms and then there were two larger rooms that served the purpose as hospital rooms.

"Howdy, Partner," Lucas said as he stuck his head through the door. "May I come in?"

"Sure," Deke said as he continued to look out the window.

"What's the matter? Are they not feedin' you anything?"

"Oh, yeah, I'm eating quite well." Deke looked toward Lucas. "The doc says I'm in a hell of a mess."

"Does that mean you're going to lose your leg?"

"Not yet, but that could be next. He said I've got gangrene, but if I stay here and let Julia and him take care of me, it may come out all right," Deke said. "The doc's gone now to get me a pint of the best whiskey he can buy from Nippy Jones."

"You plannin' on getting' drunk while you're here?" Lucas asked, trying to lighten the mood.

"I wish," Deke said. "The doc's getting' ready to do what he calls debridement, and he sort of hinted that it might hurt a little bit."

"That's not a procedure I know," Lucas said.

"Well, he's going to go in and cut all the dead tissue away. You want to stay and help?" Deke asked as he smiled at Lucas.

"I don't think so," Lucas said. "I think I'll just take a swig of your whiskey and find a seat outside."

"Coward," Deke said.

Just then Dr. Simpson and Julia came into the room.

"Marshal, I'm glad you're here. Deke could use someone to hold him down while we do this."

"It's gonna be that bad, Doc," Deke said.

"I'll not sugarcoat it, it's bad."

"Are you going to do it right now?" Lucas asked, hoping that he would have an opportunity to leave.

"The sooner, the better," Dr. Simpson said. He handed

the bottle of whiskey to Deke. "Drink as much as you want, son."

Deke handed the bottle to Lucas. "You first."

Lucas took a swallow of the whiskey then handed it back to Deke where he promptly drained the bottle.

"You stand behind him and make certain he doesn't jerk around or try to get up," Dr. Simpson said. The doctor was already at the basin where he had thoroughly washed his hands and was now pouring some carbolic acid over them.

"You might want to put this over your nose and mouth," Julia said as she handed Lucas a long strip of bandage.

Lucas took the cloth, not sure why he needed anything when neither the doctor nor Julia had any covering on their faces.

"Are we ready," Dr. Simpson said as he moved toward Deke. "Julia, start soaking the dressing in carbolic acid. We might need quite a few bandages."

"Yes, sir," Julia said.

Lucas moved to his position. When the dressing was removed, he became aware of why Julia had given him a face covering. The odor coming from the wound was overpowering, and it was all Lucas could do to keep from throwing up. Deke's leg was a purplish color and the sight of the break was shiny and swollen.

The first thing Dr. Simpson did was to pour carbolic acid onto the wound. That alone caused Deke to scream in agony. He began to writhe and it was all Lucas could do to hold him in place.

"Julia, get some chloroform. I didn't want to use it unless I had to, but I can't risk causing more damage. And, Marshal, if you want to step out of the room, I won't need you now."

Lucas nodded as he headed for the door. When he got outside, he began retching.

When Dr. Simpson came out about an hour later, Lucas was sitting in a chair on the front porch of the office.

"I'm sorry about that," Dr. Simpson said, "but I wanted you to see just how bad an injury Deke has. You have to help me convince him that he has to stay here at least through the summer."

"I understand," Lucas said. "I'll do what I can, but Deke is a stubborn man."

Lucas made his way to Nippy Jones Tavern. He stepped up to the bar.

"Marshall, what'll it be?" the bartender asked.

"Whiskey—make it a double," Lucas said.

The bartender furrowed his brow. "Trouble?"

"You could say that. My partner's in a bad way."

"Pauley. The doc said he was tryin' to save his leg, when he bought him a pint today," the bartender said. "You say he's your partner?"

"Yeah, has been for about a year now," Lucas said.

"You might not want advice from a backwater barkeep, but if I was you, I'd move on."

Lucas took a sip of his whiskey. "And why do you say that?"

"If you stay around here, why Pauley'll be wantin' to get up and get goin'," the bartender said. "Especially if he thinks he's holdin' you back."

Lucas took another drink as he looked the bartender directly in the eyes.

"Just sayin'," the bartender said as he moved on down

the bar.

When Lucas was finished with his drink, he went to see Sheriff Mason.

"Marshall, don't tell me you liked your accommodations so much that you want to spend another night with me?" the sheriff teased.

"Not hardly," Lucas said as he rubbed his still scruffy beard. "What I need is a hot bath and a shave."

"Tubby Waggoner's the man to see, and if you don't want to spend another night with me, his wife keeps a clean boarding house behind his shop," the sheriff said. "I think she keeps rooms for them that want to stay a long time—if that's what you're a plannin' to do." A grin crossed the sheriff's face.

"You know I'm not stayin' in San Martin," Lucas said.

"You mean the stunt Doc Simpson pulled on you worked?"

"I don't know what you're talking about. What stunt?"

"Ever'body knows old Doc wasn't gonna cut no proud flesh out of a man, unless he put him out," the sheriff said.

"Well, it worked," Lucas said. "Do you have the dodgers for Babcock and Gibson?"

"Right here, handy," Sheriff Mason said as he pulled them out of his top drawer.

"You knew I'd be back?"

"I did. I know your kind. When someone needs to be brought to justice and you might be the one who could do it, you'll not hang back. Am I right?"

"I suppose so," Lucas said as he picked up the wanted posters. "Are these for me?"

"Yeah. I got others. Is Pauley all right with you goin' on?"

"I've not told him yet," Lucas said. "I figure he's got one hell of a headache about now."

LUCAS HAD A RESTLESS NIGHT. He had taken the words of the bartender and the sheriff to heart, but he still felt he was betraying Deke Pauley by not staying in San Martin until he was able to ride. On the other hand, he knew if the situation was switched around, Deke would go after Babcock and Gibson. A one-thousand-dollar reward for each of the two men would be hard to turn down for a true bounty hunter.

Lucas had stayed at the Waggoner boarding house and he had gone into the dining room when Sheriff Mason came in.

"Mornin' Marshall, care if I join you?" he said.

"Sure," Lucas said as he pushed out a chair with his foot. "I was just goin' to get some breakfast."

At that moment, Tubby Waggoner brought two cups of coffee to the table.

"Are you gents fixin' to eat breakfast this mornin'?"

"That we are," Sheriff Mason said. "What's Bertha got in the oven?"

"She'll have sorghum biscuits comin' right out. Since the marshal here is our only guest this mornin', she put on a little extra."

"That sounds good," Lucas said. "Put a couple of fried eggs with that and I'll be fine."

"There's more than that," Tubby said, "and my Bertha will be some put out if you don't eat her grits. She got up early to grind the hominy."

Lucas smiled. "What else will there be?"

"Fresh antelope steak," Tubby said. "Now, that's some fine eatin'!"

"I'll tell you what," Lucas said. "Why don't you bring the sheriff and me whatever Bertha wants us to eat."

Tubby patted Lucas on his shoulder. "You're a good man, Marshal."

When Tubby left the table, Lucas turned to the sheriff. "Is that how it usually works?"

"Yep, it is. Wait'll you taste her sorghum biscuits. They're somethin' special."

When they finished eating, Lucas and the sheriff went through the barbershop and came out on the street.

"Have you told Pauley you're going after Babcock and Gibson?" the sheriff asked.

"Not yet, but I'm headed over that way now," Lucas said. "About the reward money that's due us for bringin' in Sanford and the other two—I want Deke to get it all."

"Damn, Cain that's crazy," the sheriff said. "You're givin' that man three thousand dollars! Do you know how many months—no how many years it would take me to earn that much money? It's a lot of money."

"I know, but Deke and I have worked well together. And Sheriff, I'm not hungry," Lucas said.

"Then it's your conscience talkin', ain't it? That's how you're justifyin' leavin' him behind."

"Maybe a little of that," Lucas said. "I'm not going to tell him when I say I'm movin' on. You'll see that he gets the money, won't you?"

"I will, but if I was bent that way, it'd be awful temptin' to keep your half," the sheriff said.

"But you aren't like that," Lucas said as he extended his hand to shake. "Besides when I bring Babcock and Gibson in, if you didn't give Deke the money, I'll find out, and then what will I do?"

"Kick my ass, that's what," Sheriff Mason said as he chuckled. Then he got sober. "What if Pauley don't make it?"

"Didn't you say Babcock took the money the town had raised to build a church? If Deke dies of natural causes, then give the money to the church."

"What if he don't die of natural causes?"

"Then give it to the church anyway."

While Lucas had been trying to sleep, the conversation he would have with Deke had played over in his mind. As he walked from the Waggoner place, he tried to call up how he had decided to approach the subject, but nothing would come to him. He didn't know why he was having such a hard time with this. It wasn't as if he and Deke had been friends forever, in fact at one time, they had been competitors going after the same bounties.

It was said that Deke had a fast draw but in the year they had been together, the occasion had not occurred where it was necessary for either of them to face off an adversary. On each apprehension, they had been able to get the drop on the men they were after.

Lucas knew he, too, was fast, but with Deke as his backup, he had let that skill slide. Over the next few months, he would have to once again sharpen his quick draw. In his line of work, one never knew when it would be necessary to save a life, whether it was his own or someone else's. It was in this state of mind that Lucas climbed the steps to Dr. Simpson's office.

Julia Simpson had a feather duster and she was carefully using it on all the pieces of furniture in the small waiting room.

"Good morning Marshall," she said as she smiled at him. "You just have to wonder how all this dirt gets into a tiny room like this."

"More 'n likely it comes in with the likes of me and my ilk," Lucas said. "How's your patient today? In a better mood, I hope."

"Oh, yes," Julia said. "If having an appetite is any indication that he's feeling better, he'll be out of here in no time."

"In no time? What does that mean? Next week? Next month? What does your father think?"

"Oh, I mean that he may be able to move down to the Waggoner's place in a while," Julia said. "I would think that would be more pleasant than being here in Dad's office, and besides, we need the room for other people."

"I see. But you would still be treating him," Lucas said.

"I'm changing the bandages three times a day now," Julia said. "I would hope when he leaves, it will eventually get down to just once a day."

"That would make it better for you. Is he awake?"

"I believe so," Julia said. "Just go on back."

When Lucas walked into the room, Deke's leg was suspended from the ceiling with a pulley and ropes.

"Wow!" Lucas said. "That's some contraption you've got there. Do you have to leave your leg elevated all the time?"

"It would seem so," Deke said. "I guess I can get out of here as soon as I can stand on my own."

"Has the doc said when that would be?"

"Naw, but let me tell you, as soon as I can walk out to the toilet, I'm out of here. Do you know how embarrassin' it is for that sweet Julia to have to take care of me? It's damned embarrassin'.

"I can imagine that," Lucas said, trying to suppress a smile.

"I've been layin' here thinkin' about somethin'," Deke said. "You remember when we formed Cain and Pauley? We said we could get out of it anytime either of us wanted to quit."

"I do remember that," Lucas said.

"Well, I want to quit," Deke said. "It's not fair to you to have to stay around San Martin till I get out of this mess I've got. You was on your own a lot more years than what we've been partners. And with my half of the reward money we'll get from bringin' in Sanford, Murphy, and Puckett, why I'll be fine to just stay here for a bit."

"It's funny you should bring this up, because I've been thinking the same thing," Lucas said. "Sheriff Mason ate breakfast with me this morning. There are a couple of real outlaws that he told me about. I've been thinkin' I'll head out to see if I can pick up one of their trails. And the good thing is, if I do catch up with either one of them, I'll have to bring them back to San Martin. If you're still here, and you're up to it, we can head out again."

"I don't know about that," Deke said. "This accident has made me start thinkin'. I've about decided I want to find some other way to make a livin'."

"What would you want to do?" Lucas asked.

"Who knows?" Deke laughed. "Maybe I'll go back East and be a bodyguard for some rich bastard, or maybe I'll hire on a riverboat as a house gambler. When you say you're a bounty hunter that sort of limits what line of work you can get into."

"I guess that's why I say I'm a US Marshall, but we both know when it comes down to it, I'm a bounty hunter, too."

"So true, my friend, we all play our games."

Lucas started out after Babcock on his own, and once again his horse became Lucas's sole confidant.

You know, Charley Two, when Babcock went into that church and murdered both the pastor and the church cleaner, he stole one hundred and seven dollars.

"What bothers me most is that it was as if their lives were worth no more than a hundred and seven dollars."

Charley Two whickered.

"Yeah, I knew you would agree with me, I mean, after all, you're pretty smart for a horse." He patted his horse's neck.

Lucas was quite content to talk with his horse, because he considered Charley Two more as a friend than a beast of burden.

"I'll tell you this, we're goin' to find that son of a bitch," Lucas said. "And when we do, you and I are going to watch 'em hang his ass."

Lucas chuckled. "What's that you say? Charley Two? You say they'll be hangin' more 'n just his ass? You know, old friend, I think you're right. They'll be hangin' all of him, that's a fact."

Charley Two was given the 'Two' appellation because Lucas wanted to honor his previous horse who had also been named Charley.

"And the best thing about it, is he never argues with me," Lucas had told Pauley, when Deke had commented on his habit of talking to his horse.

"Are you trying to make me believe that your best friend is a horse?" Pauley had asked him. Lucas had told him that Charley Two did everything he asked of him and he agreed with everything Lucas said.

Lucas remembered the conversation. Deke had laughed and told him he had been chewing loco weed.

Lucas was already missing the camaraderie that had existed between him and Deke. Looking back, it was a strange relationship. Lucas had shared the pain he had felt when Rosie died and his child was lost, but Deke had never shared anything about his own personal life. Lucas didn't even know where he had grown up. In that moment, Lucas accepted that the relationship or partnership or however he wanted to think of it was over. And Lucas could accept that.

Lucas's search for Babcock had taken longer than he had expected. It was now into the spring, and with the cooler nighttime temperatures he had bought a warmer coat.

He had trailed Babcock to the Apache Mountains in West Texas, and now he was riding along Sulphur Creek. He thought that Babcock would have to stay near the creek for a source of water.

"Charley Two, let me know if you need water, because we've got plenty of it," Lucas said.

Charley Two whickered.

It wasn't just Charley Two that Lucas treated as a person. He had been the same way with Charley One, and both horses had reacted to him in a way that was beyond horse and rider.

Lucas dismounted, and as Charley Two began drinking, Lucas started filling his canteen. As he was doing so, there was a little popping splash of water, right in front of him. That was followed immediately by the sound of a gunshot. Someone was shooting at him. He slapped Charley Two on his hindquarters.

"Go!" he shouted, and as Charley Two ran away, Lucas ran up a nearby ridgeline, then rolled down over the other side to get himself out of the line of fire.

Lucas heard a cackling laugh. "Bud, you're in a world of hurt now, ain't ya? Your horse done run off on ya, you ain't got no rifle with you, 'n I'm outta pistol range."

"Don't be too sure, Babcock," Lucas called back to him. "I've chased you too far to let you get away now."

Babcock answered with another shot, and though Lucas was safely below the ridge crest, he could hear the bullet pop as it passed just overhead. Keeping below the ridge crest, Lucas began working his way closer to Babcock.

"Hey," Babcock shouted. "Look at your horse now!"

"What?" Lucas asked.

Looking back in the direction Charley Two had taken, he saw his horse coming back.

"Say goodbye to your horse," Babcock said.

"Charley, no, go back!" Lucas shouted, but even as he was calling out, he heard the sound of Babcock's rifle, and he saw Charley Two go down.

"You son of a bitch!" Lucas shouted. He started running along the ridge just below the crest, until he got to where he thought he would be even with Babcock. Climbing up to the top of the ridge, he looked down and saw Babcock holding the reins of his horse, getting ready to mount.

"Hold it, you're not going anywhere," Lucas shouted down to him.

Babcock dropped the reins and jerked his rifle around to shoot at Lucas. Babcock hurried his shot, and the bullet went wide. Lucas returned fire and saw a hole appear in Babcock's forehead. Babcock's horse turned, and galloped away.

Lucas hurried to the spot where Charley Two had fallen. As he approached, he saw Charley Two's stomach moving, and he heard the wheezing as the horse struggled to breathe. Lucas knew that the wound was fatal.

"Oh, no, Charley, oh no, I'm so sorry about this," Lucas said, and after examining his horse for a moment, Lucas sat down beside him. He knew that the common practice would be to put him down, so he drew his pistol, cocked it, and aimed it at his head. He held the gun in place for a moment or two, but found that he couldn't do it, so he let the hammer down.

"Do people actually do this for their horses, or do they simply do it because it's more convenient for them?"

Lucas knew that Charley Two was dying, but he didn't appear to be in any acute pain.

"I'll tell you what, old friend. I'm going to stay right here, with you for as long as it takes."

Lucas scooted over closer to his horse then put Charley Two's head on his lap. He rubbed him behind his ears as he began speaking to him.

"Say, do you remember that time that you were running at a full gallop, and when you hit a creek, I got knocked out of the saddle, and you laughed at me? And the hell of it is, you did it of a pure purpose. No, don't you try and get out of it now, you know damn well you did."

Lucas continued to talk to Charley Two, as he rubbed

him behind the ears. After about an hour, Charley Two whickered a few times, then took his last breath.

"Goodbye, my dear old friend," Lucas said, as tears rolled down his cheeks. He sat there for several minutes, with a choked throat and wet cheeks, embracing Charley Two's head and leaning over so that his forehead was pressing against Charley Two's head. Finally, Lucas got up, and leaving his horse, walked over to look down at Babcock's body. He kicked Babcock in the head, even though he knew he was dead.

"I wish you could feel that, you sorry bastard."

Lucas looked around for Babcock's horse, hoping that he had come back, but the horse was nowhere to be seen.

"Looks like I'm going to have one hell of a long walk."

Lucas walked back to Charley Two. He took one, last long look at him, then he stripped him of the saddle and tack. He had crossed a railroad track about ten miles back. He wasn't sure where the track led, but it didn't make any difference, because he was going to flag down the next train, no matter which way it was going.

Lucas tossed the saddle over his shoulder and started his walk. He was leaving not only Charley Two behind, but also John Babcock. Babcock's body, would be worth the thousand-dollar bounty if he could produce it, but right now he didn't care about the money. As far as he was concerned, being food for the critters was good enough for him. He took the first step of what would be about a four-hour trek.

Babcock hadn't been his only quarry. He was also looking for Press Gibson, and the bounty for Gibson had grown even higher than it was for Babcock. As soon as he got to the next town, he'd get another horse and continue the search.

6

About four hours after starting his long walk, Lucas dropped his saddle with a sigh of relief. Before him, empty railroad tracks stretched out like black ribbons across the bleak landscape, reaching from horizon to horizon. For the moment they gave as little comfort as the barren sand, rocks, and cactus of the desert itself, but Lucas knew that the railroad was his salvation, and he was sure that a train would be through before nightfall.

Of the two men that he was after, the reason Lucas had gone after Babcock first was because he had a strong lead as to where he might be. He had found Babcock, but because he left Babcock's body as food for the critters, he would not be able to collect the bounty.

He didn't really care that he wouldn't be able to collect the bounty. For Lucas, the reward was that he had killed the son of a bitch who had killed Charley Two.

Now he would turn his attention to Press Gibson. Besides the known killing of the man over a poker game, Lucas knew Gibson had recently attempted a bank robbery, where he had shot down a teller and two customers. One of the customers had been a woman who was about to give birth.

The state government, the town, and the bank president had all offered rewards so that the unpleasant gentleman was now worth fifteen hundred dollars to anyone who could bring him in...dead or alive. Lucas intended to have that reward.

Lucas would by now be well on the trail of Gibson, if it hadn't taken so long to find Babcock. Now, with Charley Two gone, there would be more delays. He knew he had walked at least ten miles, carrying his saddle with him. Now all that was left for Lucas to do was catch the train. So, using his saddle and his coat as a pillow, he lay down beside the tracks to wait.

DEKE PAULEY STUDIED the town as he rode in. It was a fairly typical West Texas town, with two, obvious divisions between the Mexican side and the American side. Pauley had actually been in this town before. Originally called Clear Springs, it was still shown that way on some maps, though the town had been renamed, and was now called Tudway.

Tudway was little more than a fly-blown speck on the wide-open range. It had seen its best days when it was called End of Track, a "hell on wheels," with enough cafés, saloons, and bawdy houses to take care of the men who were building the railroad. As the railroad continued on its westward trek, however, Tudway lost most of its original population base. Its citizenship was made up of Americans and Mexicans, and the little town was hanging on, waiting for the eventual prosperity the railroad promised.

Deke rode into town slowly, sizing it up as he did so. The northeast side of the town was the American side. It was made up of whipsawed lumber shacks with unpainted, splitting wood turning gray. The southwest side of town was the Mexican end of town, and it was dominated by sand-colored adobe buildings.

Deke stopped in front of the Golden Eagle Saloon. He maneuvered his leg off his horse, then tied his horse off at the hitch rail. He got up the steps and then went inside. Although he had seen few people outside, and even fewer frequenting any of the stores or shops, there were more than he expected in the saloon. Most were engaged in half a dozen conversations, but a few of the customers glanced his way.

The bartender greeted him. "What'll it be?"

"A beer."

The bartender drew the mug and set it before him.

"What happened to this town?" Deke asked. "The last time I was here, it seemed to be quite a bit livelier than it is now."

"Yeah, well if you recall, it was End of Track then, so we had quite a few of the track layers with us."

"Yeah, now that you mention it, it was End of Track, wasn't it?"

BY AN UNEXPECTED COINCIDENCE, Press Gibson came riding into Tudway at that very moment. Always on the lookout for possible lawmen or bounty hunters, Gibson perused the town and everyone on the street.

There was one, rather substantial-looking brick

building with a sign over the door that identified it as the BANK OF TUDWAY. Gibson figured the bank might offer some promise. He had only gotten two hundred and fifteen dollars from his last job and, in frustrated rage over such slim pickings, had shot the teller. It would have ended there if a man and woman hadn't come in at that exact moment. The woman started screaming, and her fool husband tried to pull his gun. Gibson had no choice—he had to shoot both of them as well. Now there was so much money on his head that he knew every bounty hunter in the country was looking for him.

Gibson rode up to the hitch rail in front of the Golden Eagle Saloon, dismounted, and patted his tan duster a few times, sending up puffs of gray-white dust, then walked inside. The saloon was busy but Gibson found a quiet place by the end of the bar. When the bartender moved over to him, Gibson ordered a beer, then stood there nursing it as he began to formulate a plan for robbing the bank.

At the opposite end of the bar from Press Gibson, Deke Pauley noticed Gibson's entrance.

Lucas and Deke had separated as friends. The last he had heard, Lucas was still after John Babcock.

With the money Deke had gotten from the Sanford bounty, plus was Lucas given him, he had spent the better part of the year in San Martin nursing his leg. To pass the time, he had worked on his draw. And now he knew he was faster than ever.

Even though he was no longer engaged as a bounty hunter, Deke recognized Gibson from the moment Gibson walked in, and he considered this an unexpected opportunity to make some money.

"Mr. Gibson," Deke called.

Deke saw Gibson have a small, almost imperceptive jerk of his head, but he didn't look up from his beer.

"Mr. Gibson!" Deke called again. "What's the matter? Have you gone deaf? Answer me."

Deke's voice was loud and authoritative, and everyone in the saloon recognized the challenge implied in its tone. All other conversations ceased, and the drinkers at the bar backed away so that there was nothing but clear space between Deke Pauley and Press Gibson. Even the bartender left his position behind the bar.

Gibson looked up from his beer. "Are you talking to me, mister?"

"Your name is Gibson, isn't it? Press Gibson?" Deke asked.

"I'm afraid you got me mixed up with someone else," Gibson said.

"No, I'm told that Gibson is a short, really ugly toad. I've seen paper on you. You're a bank robber and a murderer, and a low-life son of a bitch. Pull your gun out with your thumb and forefinger, and lay it on the bar. I'm taking you to jail."

"Oh, you're taking me to jail, are you?" Gibson replied. He laughed. "I don't see you wearin' a badge. Where do you come off sayin' you're takin' me to jail?"

"Because I'll be collecting the bounty on you," Deke said as if that explained everything.

"And if I say that ain't goin' to happen?"

"Oh, it's goin' to happen all right," Deker said. "I'm going to make it happen."

"Well now, is that a fact?" Gibson said. He wiped the foam from his lips with the back of his hand. "What if I tell you there's no way I'll be walkin' down to that jail with you."

"You don't have to walk down to the jail with me if you don't want to. There are other ways to get you there."

"How do you propose to do that?"

"I propose to kill you, then grab hold of your feet, and drag your ass down there," Deke said easily. There was a collective gasp from those who were watching intently as the real-life drama played out before them.

Gibson set his beer mug down, then stepped away from the bar. He flipped his duster back so that his gun was exposed. He was wearing it low and kicked out, the way a man wears a gun when he knows how to use it.

"You've got a big mouth, mister," Gibson said. "I reckon it's about time you and me got this thing settled."

Deke stepped away from the bar as well. Like Gibson, he wore his gun low and kicked out.

"What might your name be, mister?" Gibson asked.

Deke smiled at him. "Pauley," he said. "Deke Pauley."

Gibson's face, which had been coldly impassive up to this point, suddenly grew animated. His skin whitened and a line of perspiration beads broke out on his upper lip. In all the outlaw camps and hideouts, he had ever been, there were two names bandied about, held up as individuals whose paths you never wanted to cross. One was Lucas Cain. The other was Deke Pauley.

Gibson had been staying out of sight for some time, but he thought it would be safe to run into a dying town like Tudway. He never suspected he would run into Deke Pauley or any other bounty hunter or lawman.

"I-I reckon I changed my mind," Gibson said. "I was just passin' through. I reckon I'll just be goin' on, now."

Deke smiled, a cold, evil smile. "No," he said. "It's too late for that now. You brought me to the ball, Mr. Gibson. Now me and you are goin' to have to dance."

Gibson had been in shoot-outs before and he was fast. Maybe he was fast enough, especially if he had the edge of drawing first. Without another word he made his move, pulling his pistol in the blink of an eye. But Deke, whether reacting to Gibson's draw or anticipating it, had his own pistol out just a split second faster, pulling the hammer back and firing in one fluid motion. In the close confines of the barroom, the gunshot sounded like a clap of thunder.

Gibson's eyes grew wide with surprise at how fast Deke had his gun up and firing. He tried hard to beat the bullet with his own draw but he couldn't do it. Deke's shot caught Gibson in the chest, and the bank robber's eyes glazed over, even as he staggered backward, crashing against the bar, then falling flat on his back on the floor of the saloon. His gun arm was thrown to one side, and the still-unfired pistol was in his hand.

There was a moment of silence, then one of the patrons nearest Gibson went over to take a look. He turned to the others.

"He's dead, folks. He's deader'n a doornail."

"Bartender," Deke said.

"Yes, sir, Mr. Pauley?"

"Set up drinks for the house."

"Yes, *sir*, Mr. Pauley," the bartender replied, and with a happy shout, everyone in the saloon rushed to the bar to give their order.

Deke had given up being a bounty hunter, planning to find some other way of making a living. Being a bounty hunter paid well, but it had its stressful and dangerous moments, such as this showdown with Gibson.

Deke grabbed Gibson by his feet and dragged him down to the sheriff's office, leaving a path in the middle of the road. He stepped over a few piles of horse droppings, but he made no effort to pull Gibson's body around them. When he reached the sheriff's office, he left Gibson's body lying in the road.

By now word had reached Sheriff Slater as to what had happened so he was standing in the doorway when Deke arrived.

"You'll be wantin' your bounty," Slater said.

"That, I will."

"I'll get your clearance for it over at the bank. It'll take about an hour. You can wait here, or in the saloon."

"I'll wait in the saloon," Deke said.

When Deke returned to the saloon, many of the customers were still celebrating, and talking about the showdown.

"I didn't think anyone would ever get Gibson," someone said.

"Here you go, Mister Pauley," the bartender said, pouring a drink. "What you just did will bring a lot of business to the saloon, so this drink is on the house."

"Thanks."

Shortly after Deke returned to the saloon, Sheriff Slater came in with the reward money.

"What's your name?" the sheriff asked.

"Pauley. Deke Pauley."

"Damn, I should have known," the sheriff said. "You're prob'ly 'bout the best known bounty hunter in the state."

"Ex-bounty hunter," Deke said.

"What do you mean, ex-bounty hunter? You just kilt Press Gibson for a bounty, didn't you?"

"Yeah, but I wasn't looking for him. He just happened to come into the saloon while I was here. I appreciate the money, but it's not something I want to do all the time now," Deke said. "At least, not like my friend Lucas Cain."

"That's right, you and Cain are friends, aren't you? Didn't you used to be partners?"

"We were, but I sort of had a little accident that laid me up for a while."

"What kind of man is he?"

"He's as good a man as you'd ever want to meet. Even if he did fight for the North durin' the war," Deke added with a little chuckle.

"Your reward is two thousand dollars," Sheriff Slater said.

"Two thousand dollars? Damn, that's higher than I thought it was. I thought it was only fifteen hundred dollars."

"They added another five hundred dollars this week," Sheriff Slater said. "It'll more 'n likely be a couple of weeks before we get the money in, though."

"That's all right with me. I don't have anyplace else I have to be. I can wait here as long as I have to."

"Where do you plan to stay while you're here?" Sheriff Slater asked.

"I don't know. Hotel, boarding house, I haven't decided."

"I have an idea that might appeal to you," Sheriff Slater said.

Deke laughed. "You're not plannin' on rentin' me a jail cell, are you, Sheriff?"

Sheriff Slater laughed as well. "No, I hadn't thought of that, but that might be a pretty good idea. No, this would be...well, I think it would be better if the offer came to you firsthand. I tell you what, why don't you go over to the Chuckwagon, that's a restaurant just down the street. Have a cup of coffee, and maybe a piece of pie? Someone will come see you in a few minutes."

Sheriff Slater wrote out a little note and handed it to Pauley. "Give this to Agnes, the coffee and pie will be on the town."

"All right, I'm not goin' to turn down free coffee and a piece of pie."

The Chuckwagon was about half a block down from the sheriff's office, and across the street. Deke was assailed by enticing aromas as soon as he stepped inside.

"Sit anywhere you want," a rather heavy-set, gray-haired woman invited.

"Are you Agnes?"

"I am."

Deke gave her the note Sheriff Slater had given him. She read it, then smiled.

"We have apple and blueberry. Which will it be?"

"Apple, I think."

DEKE WAS JUST FINISHING his pie when a tall, well-dressed man with a neatly trimmed mustache and dark hair, laced with gray came over to talk to him.

"Would you be Deke Pauley?" the man asked.

"I am."

The man smiled, and extended his hand. "I'm Jules Tudway."

"Tudway, like the name of the town?" Pauley asked.

Tudway smiled. "Yes, since I own the town, it only seems right that it would be named for me."

Deke chuckled.

"Do you find that funny, sir?" Tudway asked, the smile gone from his lips.

"No, it's just that I've never met anyone who actually owns a whole town before," Deke said. "I'm impressed."

"Impressed enough to come work for me?" Tudway asked.

"Work for you? What would you want me to do?"

"It is only natural that an operation as large as Tudway Enterprises would have enemies, enemies that would like to see harm come to me, and by extension, would even prefer that I be dead.

"I would like you to come work for me as head of my private security company, with the obligation of keeping my businesses, and me, safe."

"Who is the head of your security now?" Deke asked.

"That's just it, Mr. Pauley. At the present time, no such thing exists. I would expect you to form the organization and hire the people we would need. And for that task, your compensation would be quite generous."

"Just how generous?" Pauley asked.

"I need to take care of a few things first, and I want you to have some time to think it over. Come out to the ranch to see me tomorrow. I'll want you to have a look around and meet some of my hands."

"All right. I'll be there tomorrow," Deke said.

7

Thirty-five miles east of Tudway, Lucas Cain was unaware that his next quarry had already been caught. Lucas was still waiting for the train, and he waited for three hours before it finally appeared. When first he saw it, it was approaching at about twenty miles per hour, a respectable enough speed, through the vastness of the desert made it appear as if the train was going much slower. Against the great panorama of the desert, the train seemed puny, and even the smoke that poured from its stack made but a tiny mark upon the big, empty skies.

Lucas could hear the train quite easily now, the sound of its puffing engine carrying to him across the wide, flat ground the way sound travels across water. He stepped up onto the track and began waving. When he heard the steam valve close and the train begin braking, he knew that the engineer had spotted him and was going to stop. As the engine approached it gave some perspective as to how large the desert really was, for the train that had appeared so tiny before was now a behemoth, blocking out the sky. It ground to a reluctant halt, its stack puffing black smoke, and its driver wheels wreathed in tendrils of white steam.

The engineer's face appeared in the open cab window. Lucas felt a prickly sensation and realized that someone was holding a gun on him. He couldn't see it, but he knew that whoever it was, probably the firemen, had to be hiding in the tender.

"What do you want, mister? Why'd you stop us?" the engineer asked.

Lucas took his hat off and brushed his hair out of his eyes. The hair was dirty-blonde, lank, and grained like oak, worn trail-weary long, just over his ears. With it repositioned, he put his hat, sweat-stained and well-worn, back on his head.

"My horse went down," he explained. "I need a ride."

The engineer studied him for a moment as if trying to ascertain whether or not Lucas represented any danger to him or to his passengers. Finally, he decided it would be safe to pick up this stranger.

"All right," the engineer said. "A dollar will get you into Clear Springs."

"Clear Springs?"

"I mean Tudway," the engineer corrected. "Ever since that fella bought the town and changed the name, I keep forgettin' to call it by its new handle. Anyhow, we'll be there in about two more hours. Take the second car. The first car is a private one, belonging to Mrs. Davenport."

"Thanks," Lucas said. He picked up the saddle and started toward the rear of the train. "Oh, and you can tell your firemen it's all right to come out now."

"What the hell? How did you know I was in here?" the firemen's muffled voice called.

Lucas knew because his very life often depended upon his ability to interpret such things.

The private car was the first car behind the tender. It was a beautifully varnished car, bearing a brass plaque with the neatly lettered words DAVENPORT COURT. Lucas had no idea what Davenport Court meant, but figured it had something to do with the Mrs. Davenport the engineer had mentioned.

As Lucas walked by the car, he saw the curtains part and a woman's face appear in one of the windows. It was the face of an older woman, with white hair and wrinkles in what was still a handsome face. She had clear, blue eyes and she appraised Lucas in frank curiosity, refusing to look away when Lucas looked back at her.

When Lucas reached the car just behind Mrs. Davenport's car, he threw his saddle up onto the deck of the vestibule then stepped inside. There were a couple of dozen passengers in the car—men, women, and children—and they all looked up in curiosity at the man who had caused the train to stop in the middle of the desert. Lucas touched the brim of his hat, then walked to the last seat on the right and settled into it. He pulled his legs up so that his knees were resting on the seat back in front of him, reached up and casually tipped his hat forward, then folded his arms across his chest. Within moments, he was sound asleep.

8

The train Lucas had flagged down had been underway for a little over an hour when it suddenly ground to a shuddering, screeching, banging halt. It stopped so abruptly that some of the passengers were thrown from their seats and a little boy, who had been running up and down the aisle, fell and began crying.

"What is it?" someone asked.

"Are we going to stop at every rock and cranny in this entire desert?" another wanted to know.

"I nearly broke my neck! The railroad is certainly going to hear from me," a man complained.

Though he could see nothing, Lucas knew at once what was going on, and he pulled his pistol from his holster, let it rest on his knee, and covered it with his hat.

"Everyone stay in your seats!" a man shouted, bursting into the car from the front. He wore a bandanna tied across the bottom half of his face, and he held a pistol that he pointed toward the passengers in the car.

"See here! What is this?" a man shouted indignantly. He started to get up, but the gunman moved quickly toward him and brought his pistol down sharply over the man's head. The passenger groaned and fell back. A woman who had been sitting with him cried out in alarm.

"Anybody else?" the gunman challenged. "Maybe you folks didn't hear what I said. I said, everyone stay in your seats."

Another gunman came in to join the first. "What happened?" he asked.

"Nothing I can't handle. Is everything under control out there?"

"Yeah," the second gunman answered. "Ever'one is doin' just what you told 'em to do."

"All right then, just get on into the next car behind us," the first gunman said. "Keep ever'one in their seats back there."

"How will I know when you're pullin' the private car away? I mean, what if you fellas leave and I don't know you're gone? I'll be stuck back there."

"We'll blow the whistle before we go. Now, get on back there like I told you."

As the second gunman started down the aisle to go to the next car, he looked over and saw Lucas then gasped.

"Hey, Tim! Look out! I believe this here is that Lucas Cain, fella!" he called, bringing his gun around toward Lucas.

"How do you know?"

"I seen 'im before."

Lucas had intended to wait for a more opportune moment, but the fat was in the fire now. He had no choice. He shot first, his bullet blasting a hole through his own hat. The gunman who had recognized him went down with a hole in his chest.

The gunman up front, the one called Tim, managed to get off a shot but he was shooting fast and wild and his bullet smashed through the window beside Lucas's seat, sending out a stinging spray of glass, but doing no other damage. Lucas brought his own pistol around and squeezed off a second shot. Tim staggered back, his hands to his throat. Blood spilled through his fingers, and he pulled his hands away. He stared at them stupidly as he went down.

During the gunfire, women screamed and men shouted. As the car filled with the gun smoke of the three discharges, Lucas scooted out through the back door of the car, jumped from the steps down to the ground, then fell and rolled out into the darkness.

"Tim! Johnny! What's goin' on in there?" someone called. "What's goin' on?"

In the dim light that spilled through the car windows, Lucas saw the gunman who was yelling at the others. This must have been the man who had been covering the engineer, and now he was moving quickly toward the back of the train. As he ran through the little golden patches of light it had the effect of a lantern blinking on and off so that first he was in shadow, then brightly illuminated...then shadow...then illuminated. Lucas aimed at him.

"Hold it right there!" Lucas called out to him. "I've got you covered. Put down your gun and throw up your hands."

"What the hell?" the bandit responded. He suddenly realized he was in a patch of light and moved quickly into the shadow to fire at Lucas. He may have thought he had found safety in the darkness, but the two-foot-wide muzzle flash of his pistol gave Lucas an ideal target and Lucas returned fire. The outlaw's bullet whistled by harmlessly, but Lucas's bullet found its mark and the would-be train robber let out a little yell, grabbed his chest, then collapsed.

Lucas stood up then and moved toward the side of the train to try to get a bead on the one who had been disconnecting the rest of the train from the private car. Lucas saw him then, just as he was stepping through the door and into the private car. Lucas snapped off a shot but missed. He saw his bullet send up sparks as it struck part of the metal in the doorframe. Lucas didn't get a second shot because the outlaw made it inside.

Lucas hurried to the front end of the same passenger car he had been riding in, then backed up against the side of it so that the robber, who was now safely inside the private car, wouldn't have a clear shot at him. One of the passengers poked his head out to see what was going on.

"Get back inside!" Lucas shouted gruffly. "You want your fool head shot off?"

The passenger jerked his head back in quickly.

Lucas peered cautiously around the corner, trying to see his adversary.

"You may as well come on out of there, there's nowhere for you to go," Lucas called. "The others are all dead. You're the only one left."

There was no answer to Lucas's demand.

"Come on out," Lucas said again. "I promise you, you aren't going to get away."

"Hey, fella. Who the hell are you?" the outlaw in the car yelled.

"The name is Cain," Lucas called back.

"Cain? *Marshal Lucas Cain?*" The outlaw's voice suddenly took on a new and more terrified edge.

"That's my name," Lucas admitted. "What is your name?"

"It's Mills. What the hell are you sayin' you're comin' after me, 'n you don't even know my name? What are you doin' here? How did you know about this? How'd you know we was comin' after the Davenport woman?"

"I'm running out of patience," Lucas said.

There was a beat of silence, then Mills called out again. "All right, I'm comin' out," he said. "Don't shoot, Cain, I'm comin' out."

Lucas watched the back door of the private car. A second later, it opened, and true to his promise, Mills came out. What he had not said, however, was *how* he was coming out. He was pushing a woman before him, and he was holding his pistol against her temple.

"You out here, Cain?" Mills called, searching the darkness. "You out here?"

"I'm here," Lucas answered. He stepped out so the outlaw could see him, and he raised his pistol to point it at Mills. "Let her go, Lucas said.

"Like hell I will," Mills replied. "This is my ticket out of here. You know who this is, don't you? This here is Mrs. Davenport. I don't guess you'd like to see her brains blowed out, would you?"

"It doesn't much matter to me, I don't even know who she is," Lucas said laconically. "What's going on between us right now has nothin' to do with the woman. She doesn't mean anything to me."

"What are you talking about? This is Leah Davenport. Do you understand what I'm saying to you? This is Leah Davenport of Davenport Court."

"Never heard of her, never heard of Davenport

Court," Lucas said. "Put your gun down. That's the only way you're going to get out of here alive."

"No, it ain't the only way I'm goin' to get out of here. I told you. I got me an ace up my sleeve."

"You've got nothin', Lucas said.

"I've got the woman."

"Yeah, so you said. What the hell is that supposed to mean to me?"

"Don't you understand, you ignorant bastard? I'm going to *shoot* her," Mills warned.

"All right, go ahead, just quit talking about it. Get it over with so you and I can get down to business."

"What?" Mills asked, shocked by the answer he hadn't expected to hear.

"I said go ahead. Do it. Shoot her," Lucas said. "With her out of the way, it'll give me an easier shot at you."

"You're bluffing."

"Think so?" Lucas asked. "All right, if you won't shoot her, *I* will. Then I'll shoot you." Lucas moved the barrel of his gun slightly so that he was now aiming at the woman. Slowly and deliberately, he cocked his pistol.

"You son of a bitch! You're crazy! You know that? You're crazy!" Mills shouted. He pulled his gun away from the woman's head so he could aim at Lucas. That was just the opening Lucas was looking for. Quickly and smoothly, Lucas moved his sight to a new target and squeezed the trigger. The gun boomed and bucked in his hand, and his bullet whizzed by within an inch of Mrs. Davenport's head, hitting the outlaw in his right eye. The impact of the heavy bullet threw him back against the door of the car, then he collapsed in a heap onto the vestibule floor. Mrs. Davenport never said a word, though she did jump involuntarily as her assailant fell behind her.

"Are you all right, ma'am? Lucas asked. He was still holding his pistol out in front of him and smoke curled up from the end of the barrel.

"Yes, I'm fine, thank you," Mrs. Davenport replied. It was the first word Lucas had heard her say. "You are one hell of a shot, Mr. Lucas Cain," she added.

Despite himself, Lucas smiled. "And you are one hell of a woman, Mrs. Davenport," he replied.

By now, the conductor had left the train and he was joined by a few of the braver passengers. Even the engineer and fireman were on the ground and they began milling around, looking at the two bodies that were outside the train.

"There are two dead inside and two dead out here. Any more left that you know of?" the conductor asked the engineer.

"No," the engineer replied. "There was just the four of 'em stopped me."

"Why'd you stop?"

"Didn't have no choice," the engineer replied. "They put a barricade across the tracks." The engineer looked at a couple of the stronger-looking passengers. "You two men want to bear a hand till we get the tracks cleared."

"Sure thing," one of them answered, and both passengers went to the front of the train with the engineer and fireman to begin clearing the cut timber from the track.

"Are you all right, Mrs. Davenport?" the conductor asked.

"Yes, thank you," Mrs. Davenport said. "I'm fine."

"No thanks to you," the conductor added, scolding Lucas. "I heard you from inside the car. What did you mean telling that man that if he didn't shoot her, you would? That was the cruelest, most inhuman, most—"

"Brilliant," Mrs. Davenport added, interrupting the conductor's tirade.

"Brilliant?" the conductor asked. He looked up at Mrs. Davenport, who was still standing on the rear vestibule of her private car. "See here, Mrs. Davenport, you aren't telling me you *approve* of what this man did, are you?"

"Yes, I'm telling you exactly that."

"But how could you?"

"Mr. Morehead, four men stopped this train," Mrs. Davenport explained. "Four men, with the intention of severing my car from the rest of the train, then taking me to who-knows-where for who-knows-what foul purpose. These four men are now dead because Mr. Cain killed them, and I am still here, safe and sound, you see."

"But the way he treated you," Morehead protested. "He showed a total disregard for your safety."

"Yes, and in so doing, denied this brigand the opportunity to use me as a shield," Mrs. Davenport replied. "I think Mr. Cain should be commended for his quick thinking, not condemned."

"Well, if that's the way you feel."

"That's the way I feel," Mrs. Davenport said. She looked down at the outlaw's twisted body. "Now, would you please get this riffraff off the back of my car? I don't intend that he should ride here all the way into Tudway."

"Yes, yes, of course," Morehead answered. "You men, get this man's body and the one out there and take them both to the rear of the train."

"What are we goin' to do with 'em, Mr. Morehead?" someone asked.

"We'll turn them over to the undertaker as soon as we reach Tudway."

"Conductor, before we turn them over to the undertaker, I'd like the sheriff to see them," Cain said.

"Whatever for?"

"I killed them," Lucas said flatly. "If there is any money on their miserable hides, it belongs to me, and I aim to collect it."

"Good heavens, man, have you no decency? I don't know where you come from, mister," Morehead said, "but around here, we show a little more respect for our womenfolk than to talk about such things as bounty money in front of them."

"Oh, for heaven's sake, Mr. Morehead, don't be ridiculous," Mrs. Davenport said. "Mr. Cain shot them, why shouldn't he be entitled to collect his reward if there is one?"

"Yes, ma'am, if you say so," Morehead replied, obviously frustrated by Mrs. Davenport's defense of Cain and chastised by her scolding tone. "All right, come along, men, let's get a move on it," he ordered gruffly, taking his frustration out on the volunteers. "We can't stay out here all night. We have to be in Tudway in an hour."

Lucas started to get back into the same car he had been riding in, but Mrs. Davenport leaned out over the wrought-iron railing of her vestibule and called out to him.

"Mr. Cain, I have liquor in my car, if you'd care to join me."

"Thanks all the same, ma'am," Lucas said, touching the brim of his hat. He nodded toward the car he had been riding in. "It'd probably be best if I just go on back where I was."

"What's the matter? You afraid of putting a bigger burr in the conductor's saddle?" Mrs. Davenport asked.

"No, ma'am. It's not that," Lucas replied.

"What is it then?" Mrs. Davenport chuckled. "I know. When I invited you for something to drink, you probably thought I was talking about elderberry wine, didn't you?"

Lucas looked at her. He *had* thought that and his slow smile gave him away.

"Uh-huh, I thought so," Mrs. Davenport said. "Well, Mr. Cain, I'll have you know that this is real sipping whiskey," she said. "Now, come on into my car and have a drink with me."

Lucas's smile broadened and he turned toward the private car.

"Yes, ma'am," he said. "If it's sipping whiskey you're talking about, then I don't mind if I do join you."

When he stepped into Mrs. Davenport's private car, he saw that the car was a luxurious oasis on wheels, a haven of opulence that stood in stark contrast to the rugged terrain outside. Polished mahogany paneling adorned the walls, reflecting the warm glow of brass fixtures. Plush velvet drapes framed the large panoramic windows, allowing glimpses of the untamed landscape.

The flickering light of crystal chandeliers cast a soft glow over the room, adding to the air of refined decadence.

Mrs. Davenport awaited Lucas with a gracious smile. She was an imposing figure, regal and composed, dressed in a gown that spoke of wealth and refinement. Her graying hair was elegantly coiffed, and a string of pearls adorned her neck.

"Mr. Cain, I cannot thank you enough for coming to my aid," Mrs. Davenport said, her voice tinged with gratitude. "Please, join me. Malcolm, fetch our guest a glass of sipping whiskey."

Malcolm, the valet, stood nearby, ever watchful in his impeccable attire, complete with a perfectly tied bowtie and white gloves.

Lucas accepted the invitation, settling into a cushioned chair opposite Mrs. Davenport. The crystal glasses clinked as Malcolm poured a rich amber liquid from an ornate decanter. The scent of aged whiskey wafted through the air, adding another layer of sophistication to the surroundings.

"I must say, Mrs. Davenport, this is the finest private car I've ever set foot in," Lucas remarked, raising his glass in a silent toast before taking a sip. The whiskey was smooth, with a hint of smokiness that lingered on the palate.

"It was a gift from my late husband, bless his soul," Mrs. Davenport replied, her eyes momentarily glazing over with a hint of nostalgia. "He believed in traveling in style, and I've done my best to maintain that tradition."

9

As the train wheels clacked rhythmically beneath him, Lucas realized that Mrs. Davenport's car had a much gentler ride than the rough-riding car Lucas had been on.

"Please serve the gentleman, Malcolm," she said to the man Lucas had seen as soon as he came into the car.

"Yes, mum," the man replied with a strong accent.

Lucas drank the whiskey he was served. Since being released from the hellhole of Andersonville, the Confederate Prison of War, Lucas had drunk just about every type of alcohol available in every saloon from Missouri to the Mexican border to the South Dakota Badlands. He had drunk beer that was so green he could still taste the yeast and whiskey that was aged with rusty nails and flavored with tobacco juice. Once he had even drunk champagne, but he had never tasted anything like the "sipping whiskey" he was drinking now.

"Do you like it?" Mrs. Davenport asked.

"Yes, ma'am," Lucas said. His answer wasn't adequate

to express how much he really did like it, but he never was a man for words.

"It comes directly from Scotland," Mrs. Davenport explained. "My late husband used to say that it was the morning mist, bottled right from the Scottish moors. Do you agree?"

Lucas shrugged and Mrs. Davenport laughed.

"I'm teasing," she said. "I don't know what the hell he meant by that either. But he was a very poetic man, my husband. He was an English man from a fine, old family who came to America and built Davenport Court." She laughed. "But then, you don't know what Davenport Court is, do you? I heard you say that to the gunman."

"No, ma'am, I don't know what it is," Lucas admitted.

"For your enlightenment, young man, Davenport Court is a cattle ranch. And not just any cattle ranch. It is a huge ranch with thousands of acres of grassland and water, and thousands of fat cows. After my husband built Davenport Court, he was like Adam in the Garden of Eden. And, like Adam, he decided that he needed to take to himself a wife. That's where I come in. He went to San Francisco to see the sights and he saw me. Your glass is empty. Pour him another, Malcolm."

"Yes, mum," Malcolm said. Malcolm, who was dressed in a coat and tails and wearing white gloves, brought the decanter of whiskey over and refilled Lucas's glass. Lucas had never actually seen anyone who dressed the way Malcolm was, and he looked at him with ill-concealed curiosity.

"Malcolm was my husband's valet," Mrs. Davenport explained. "He is what the English like to call a gentleman's gentleman," she said. "Malcolm, tell Mr. Cain how long you have been with the Davenport family."

"Oh, for over two hundred years now, sir," Malcolm answered easily.

"What? Did you just say that you had been with the Davenport family for two hundred years?" Lucas asked.

Mrs. Davenport laughed. "You don't understand the British, Mr. Cain. Malcolm doesn't mean that *he* has been with the Davenport family for two hundred years," she explained. "He means his family has served the Davenport family for two hundred years. That's how they think, you know. It's all family and tradition, and one life doesn't mean much to a family that thinks in terms of ten generations. Edward came across the ocean with Rowland."

"Rowland?" Lucas asked.

"Lord Rowland Addison Davenport. If we were in England, I'd be a lady." She laughed out loud. "But of course, we aren't in England, so I have no illusions about who or what I am."

"I think you are a fine lady," Lucas said.

"I could have been. I started out that way. I was born in Virginia to a fine, old family, but I came to California in forty-nine with my first husband. His name was Lawrence Stephens and he had big plans to get rich in the gold fields, then go back and buy a large tobacco plantation. But what he got was killed by a claim jumper. I went to work in a saloon. I'll skip through the rest of the story and just say that that was where I was when Rowland saw me." Mrs. Davenport tossed the rest of her drink down, then wiped her mouth with the back of her hand. "Does it shock you to know that I once earned my keep by drinking with drunken miners?"

"Why should that shock me?" Lucas asked. "You're a very handsome lady. I can see why miners, or anyone else for that matter, would enjoy having a drink with you. As I am now."

Mrs. Davenport laughed out loud. "You know what you are, Mr. Cain? You are what we girls used to call a golden-tongued warbler," she said. "Yes, sir, you really are. And you are so good that it doesn't even seem like you're just trying to flatter me. I actually think you mean it."

"I do mean it," Lucas said easily.

Mrs. Davenport stared at him through narrowed eyes for a long moment. "I figure you also know that every now and then I did more than just drink with those fellas. But there you sit, passing no judgment. You're a good man, Lucas Cain. You're as good a man as my Rowland, and that's saying a lot. And you saved my life tonight, and for that, I would like to reward you."

"No need," Lucas said. "I expect there's paper on those four galoots. When we get into Tudway, I'll get my reward from the sheriff. At any rate, I'm about to start trailing someone and I expect I'll catch up with him soon. When I do, there will be a good payday in it for me."

"Who are you chasing?"

"A man named Press Gibson."

"I read something about him, I believe. He murdered a poor pregnant woman, didn't he?"

"I'm not completely up to date on all of his escapades, but I wouldn't put anything past him," Lucas replied.

"Well, I hope you do catch up with him soon, not only because I want you to get the reward but also because such a person shouldn't be allowed to run free. But what about the men you encountered tonight? Have you seen any posters on them? Do you know for a fact that they are wanted?"

"No," Lucas admitted. "But anyone who would try to rob the train has probably done something else. I'm sure there's a reward on them."

"And you are going to inquire about them from the sheriff in Tudway?"

"Yes," Lucas said.

Mrs. Davenport shook her head. "No, Mr. Cain, I don't think so," she said.

"You have a reason for thinking that way?" Lucas asked.

"Yes," Mrs. Davenport replied. "Tudway is named for Jules Tudway. And I happen to know that the men you did battle with work for Jules Tudway. If you work for Tudway, you can do anything you want and get away with it, because in the town of Tudway, and for many miles in all directions around the town, Jules Tudway writes his own law."

"And Tudway's law says you can rob trains?" Lucas asked.

"Oh, but that's just the point, you see. Those men weren't trying to rob the train, Mr. Cain. They were after me."

"Why?"

"Mr. Tudway and I are having a difference of opinion right now," Mrs. Davenport said.

"Some difference of opinion. It caused me to kill four men," Lucas said.

"From the moment they recognized you, you had no choice. They thought you were working for me and they would have killed you if they could."

THE SUN HUNG low in the Texas sky, casting long shadows across the vast plains as Deke Pauley rode toward the sprawling Winning Hand Ranch. The dust kicked up by his horse's hooves trailed behind him, marking his approach to the domain of Jules Tudway, a man whose appetite for land knew no bounds.

The Winning Hand Ranch loomed in the distance, a testament to Tudway's ruthless ambition, an ambition supported by Tudway's willingness to challenge the limits of ethics and the law. As Deke neared the ranch house, he observed the expansive fields and the cattle that grazed upon them, evidence of Tudway's relentless expansion.

Deke dismounted and tethered his horse to the hitching post, the creaking sound of the leather announcing his arrival. The air was thick with tension as he walked toward the imposing ranch house. The door swung open before he could knock, revealing the figure of Jules Tudway himself.

Standing tall and imposing, Tudway greeted Deke with a calculating smile. "I'm glad to see that you are interested enough in my proposal to see what I can offer someone who has strayed from the righteous path of the bounty hunter."

Deke's eyes met Tudway's, a silent acknowledgment of the truth. "I've strayed, but I'm not lost," Deke replied.

Tudway gestured for Deke to enter the dimly lit ranch house. The smell of cigar smoke hung in the air as they settled into Tudway's study, adorned with maps displaying the vast expanse of land he aimed to conquer.

"As I told you yesterday, I've got a proposition for you, Pauley," Tudway said, pouring two glasses of whiskey. "I need a man with your skills to lead my armed guards. We're expanding, and I need someone who isn't afraid to get his hands dirty."

Deke eyed Tudway, a lingering silence hanging between them. The room seemed to close in, filled with the weight of unspoken choices.

"I don't play by your rules, Tudway," Deke finally spoke, his gaze unwavering. "But I've got my reasons. What's in it for me?"

Tudway leaned back, a sly grin playing on his lips. "You'll be getting a steady paycheck of a thousand dollars a month."

Deke caught his breath. The last time Deke had worked on a ranch, the pay was thirty dollars a month.

Tudway smiled. "You heard right, Pauley. A thousand dollars a month."

"That's quite an offer," Deke said.

"Believe me, you will have to earn it."

Deke contemplated Tudway's offer. The room seemed to echo with the ghosts of choices made and paths diverged.

"All right, Tudway," Deke said, his tone a low growl. "I reckon you've just hired yourself the devil that you need."

Tudway extended his hand, sealing the unholy pact between them.

10

As the train began to slow, Mrs. Davenport pulled the curtain open and looked outside. Lucas saw a small house slide by, its interior dimly lit by candles.

"We're coming into Tudway," she said.

"I reckon I'll be getting off here," Lucas said.

"I hope you aren't too disappointed when you find that what I said about those galoots is true. You'll find no paper on them, Lucas Cain. Not here. Probably not anywhere."

"I've got to get off here, anyway," Lucas said. "I've got to buy myself another horse somewhere, and I guess here is as good as any place. I do want to thank you for the whiskey and the company," he said. "I've never had a train trip so fine."

"You saved my life, Lucas Cain. Whiskey seems little enough payment," she said. "And as for the company, why, I expect I got more pleasure out of that than you did."

"Are you going on through?"

Mrs. Davenport smiled. "Oh no," she said. "I'll have

my car detached from the train and put on a sidetrack. I've got a little business to take care of while I'm here."

"Well, good luck, and goodbye," Lucas said. He touched his hat, nodded to Malcolm, then went out onto the vestibule to pick up his saddle. With his saddle thrown over his shoulder again, he stepped down onto the wooden platform of the Tudway depot and looked around.

Behind Lucas, the train, temporarily at rest from the long run, wasn't quiet. Because the engineer kept the steam up, the valve continued to open and close in great, heaving sighs. Overheated wheel bearings and gearboxes popped and snapped as its tortured metal cooled. On the platform all around him, there was a discordant course of squeals, laughter, shouts, and animated conversation as people were getting on and off the train.

When Lucas looked toward the rear of the train, he saw that the four bodies were being taken down from the last car and laid out side by side at the far end of the platform. Already the curious were beginning to gather around the bodies, and by the time Lucas made arrangements to leave the saddle in the baggage room of the depot, there were more than two dozen people.

"Did you see the bodies they took off the train?" the baggage clerk asked as he got out a yellow tag to tie to Lucas's saddle.

"Yeah," Lucas said. "I saw them."

"There is goin' to be hell to pay over this," the clerk said. "Those men worked for Mr. Tudway."

"Who is this fella Tudway, anyway?" Lucas asked. "I mean, other than the fact that he has a town named after him."

"Who is he? Where have you been mister that you haven't heard of Jules Tudway? He's the biggest landowner within five hundred miles in any direction. He owns Winning Hand Ranch and that's even bigger than Davenport Court. I reckon you've heard of Davenport Court, haven't you?"

"Yes," Lucas said. "I have."

"Of course, there was a time when Davenport Court was the biggest spread. Mr. Davenport owned just about all the land around, then. He was English, you know."

"So I heard. Was Davenport Court bigger than Winning Hand?"

The clerk chuckled. "Hell, Davenport owned Winning Hand too. Only it wasn't Winning Hand then. It was all just a part of his spread. Folks say that in its heyday, Davenport Court was bigger 'n anything in Texas, bigger 'n the next two combined."

"If Davenport used to own it, how did Tudway come by Winning Hand?"

"Nobody knows for sure. Tudway just come in here several years ago and chewed off enough land from Davenport to build Winning Hand. They must've had somethin' worked out, though, 'cause Davenport didn't make no fight over it. Then, after that, Tudway started addin' land to Winning Hand so that now it's bigger'n it ever was. I can tell you this, though. He's saved this town. Clear Springs was dyin'. I mean pure-dee dyin'. Stores was closein' and folks was movin' away. Mr. Tudway offered good money for all the places that was goin' out of business and sometimes that was 'bout all a family was able to salvage, just enough money to buy a ticket out of town. Then Mr. Tudway built a bank, and next thing you know we looked around and saw that he owned more'n half the town. Well, sir, since he kept the town from dyin', the town council got together and voted to change the name from Clear Springs to Tudway."

"Quite a man, your Mr. Tudway," Lucas said dryly.

"Yes, sir, he is," the clerk responded, missing the sarcasm. He dipped his pen in an inkwell, then looked up at Lucas. "What's your name?" He asked. "I need it for the tag."

"Cain."

"Cain," the clerk repeated, and he started to write the name out, then he looked up again. This time his eyes reflected fear. "Would that be Lucas Cain?" he asked.

"Cain's all you need. Where is the sheriff's office?"

"It's down the street," the clerk said. "But if you are looking for Sheriff Slater, you'll find him down there with those four dead men. This has been quite a day for him. There's these four, plus Press Gibson."

Lucas had already started toward the sheriff when he heard Gibson's name. He turned and looked back at the clerk.

"What about Press Gibson?" he asked.

"Oh, that's right, you just arrived on the train, so you couldn't know," the clerk said. "We had quite a shoot-out down at the saloon yesterday. Press Gibson made the mistake of trying to outdraw someone who was faster, and he died for his trouble."

"I hear Press Gibson was pretty fast," Lucas said.

"Oh, yes, indeed he was," the clerk agreed. "But not as fast as Deke Pauley."

"Deke Pauley? Is Pauley here?" Lucas asked as a smile crossed his face.

"Yes. Do you know him?"

"I know him," Lucas said.

"Yes, well, of course you would. I expect all you fast guns know each other. You know, I wonder which of you…" The clerk let the thought drop, then dismissed it with a weak laugh. "Well, never mind, I was only wondering, that's all. Don't give it a second thought," he said.

"I won't," Lucas replied.

Lucas walked down to the far end of the station platform, where the bodies had been laid out as if on display. Each one had his arms folded across his chest. Three of them had their eyes open. The only exception was Mills whose eyelid muscles had been destroyed by the bullet that hit him in the eye. Among the dozen or more who were standing there looking down at the bodies, one man was wearing a suit and smoking a cigar. A star, attached to the lapel of his suit jacket, identified him as the sheriff.

"There he is, Sheriff," someone said. "That's the fella that done it. He took all four of 'em on. It was quite a thing to see."

The sheriff took his cigar out of his mouth and spat out a few pieces of loose tobacco before he spoke.

"You did this?" he asked.

"Yes."

"Well," the sheriff said. "Mr. Tudway ain't goin' to like it too much. I mean me not chargin' you with murder or anything. But there's nothing I can do. I got a whole train full of witnesses who swear you kilt them in self-defense." He waved his hand. "You're free to go."

"I'd like to check your dodgers," Lucas said. "I want to see if there's any reward for these men."

"There ain't none."

"How do you know?"

"These men worked for Tudway. If they was wanted, I would have already picked them up."

"Maybe there's some paper out on them that you don't know about," Lucas suggested.

"I doubt it."

"Check."

The sheriff sighed. "I guess I can send a telegram up to the capital tomorrow mornin'," he said. "If you want to stick around until then."

"I've got no place else to go," Lucas said. "Is there a hotel in town?"

"No hotel," the sheriff answered. "You might get a room down at the Golden Eagle Saloon if the whores ain't usin' all of 'em."

"Thanks," Lucas said. "I'll stop by and see you in the morning."

"You'll be wastin' your time," the sheriff said, sticking his cigar back in his mouth.

Lucas walked down the street from the depot toward the town. The Golden Eagle was the most substantial-looking saloon in a row of saloons. There was a drunk passed out on the steps in front of the place, and Lucas had to step over him in order to go inside.

Because all the chimneys of all the lanterns were soot-covered, what light there was inside was dingy and filtered through drifting smoke. The place smelled of whiskey, stale beer, and sour tobacco. There was a long bar on the left, with dirty towels hanging on hooks about every five feet along its front. A large mirror was behind the bar, but like everything else about the saloon, it was so dirty that Lucas could scarcely see any images in it, and what he could see was distorted by imperfections in the glass.

Over against the back wall, near the foot of the stairs, a cigar-scarred, beer-stained upright piano was being played by a bald-headed musician. The tune was "Buffalo Gals" and one of the girls who *was* a buffalo gal stood alongside, swaying to the music. Lucas was once told that the song was now very popular in the East and was often sung by the most genteel ladies. The Easterners had no idea that the term *buffalo gal* referred to doxies who, during the rapid expansion of the railroad, had to ply their trade on buffalo robes, thrown out on the ground. This was because there were few buildings and fewer beds.

Out on the floor of the saloon, there were eight or ten tables, nearly all of them occupied. A half-dozen are so girls were flitting about, pushing drinks and promising more than they could ever deliver. A few card games were in progress, but most of the patrons were just drinking and talking. The subject of their conversation was the gunfight that had taken place in the saloon earlier. By now they had also heard of the gunfight that had taken place on the train, and already there was speculation as to which of the two victors was the best.

"In my mind, there ain't no doubt," one of the men at one of the tables were saying. "Cain took on four men. Four, mind you, and he kilt all four. You can't compare that with Pauley killin' just one man."

"The hell you can't," another man contended. "Cain done his killin' in the dark. Pauley done his killin' in broad daylight. He called Gibson out and stood up to him, face-to-face. And did you see Pauley's draw? Faster'n greased lightnin' it was. Why it was that quick I'd never seen nothin' more'n a jump of his shoulder and the gun was in his hand. In his hand and blazin', it was, and Gibson was graspin' his chest and fallin', already deader'n a doornail without gettin' off even one shot. Pauley's danced on many a man's grave, you can believe."

"Still, four to one," one of the others said, and the argument continued.

"I'd sure like to see them fellas go up agin each other," another said, putting to voice what all were thinking.

"Whoo-ee! Wouldn't that purely be somethin' though?"

The bartender was pouring the residue from abandoned whiskey glasses back into a bottle when Lucas stepped up to the bar. He pulled a soggy cigar butt from one glass, laid the butt aside, then poured the whiskey back into the bottle without qualms. Lucas held up his finger.

"Yeah?" the bartender responded.

"I'd like a room."

"With or without?"

"With or without what?"

The bartender looked up in surprise. "Are you kidding me, mister? With or without a woman."

"Without."

"Six bits."

"Six bits? Isn't that a little expensive?"

"If we left it empty so the girls could use it for their customers, we could make three, maybe four times that," the bartender said. "Six bits, take it or leave it."

It had been more than eighteen hours since Lucas had picked up his sleeping roll this morning. That was followed by an almost ten-mile walk, then a gunfight, then conversation and sipping whiskey with Mrs. Davenport. He hadn't really needed anything to make him sleepy, but the sipping whiskey had done just that. Six bits? Hell, he thought. He would pay six bucks to get a little sleep.

"Here," Lucas said, slapping the coins on the bar. "Tell your girls and their customers not to come into my room by mistake. If they do, they just might get shot."

"Mister, I don't know who the hell you are, but it ain't healthy to go around making threats you can't back up," the bartender said. He picked up the silver and took it over to the moneybox, then reached for a key.

"Kelly," someone said from the other end of the bar. "Kelly, come here."

The bartender went over to the customer, then leaned over as the customer whispered something in his ear. The bartender looked back toward Lucas, listened a moment longer, then visibly blanched. He hurried back down the bar with the key.

"Mr. Cain, you have a good sleep tonight. Don't you worry none about anyone disturbin' you. I'll make sure you're left in peace."

"Cain?" one of the conversationalists at the tables said, twisting around and looking toward Lucas.

"That there is Lucas Cain," another said.

All conversation halted as the entire saloon turned and looked at the man who had been one of the subjects of their discussion.

Lucas looked out over the room coldly and without comment, then he turned back to the bartender.

"And what I said a while ago. You know, 'bout not makin' no threats you can't back up? I hope you don't hold me to that, Mr. Cain," the bartender went on. "I was just shootin' off my mouth where I didn't have no right, that's all. I didn't mean nothin' by it. Here you go. It's room seven."

"Thanks," Lucas said, picking up his key.

"Not at all. It's my pleasure to serve Lucas Cain," the bartender said.

"Yes, sir," Lucas heard someone behind him say as he started up the stairs. "Lucas Cain and Deke Pauley goin' at one another. That would be somethin' to behold. Folks would come from miles around to see somethin' like that."

When Lucas got to room seven, he lit a lantern then had a look around. The room had a high-sprung, cast-iron bed, a chest, and a small table with a picture and basin. On the wall was a neatly lettered sign that read:

> DO NOT SPIT ON THE FLOOR.
> GENTLEMEN, PLEASE REMOVE SPURS WHILE IN BED.

Lucas opened the window and saw that his room looked out over the street. He heard the train whistle blow and looked down toward the depot just in time to see the train he had arrived on pulling away. Mrs. Davenport's private car, dark now, had been shunted aside and was sitting on a sidetrack, just beyond the depot building.

It was a busy night. In addition to the clanging bell and puffing steam of the departing locomotive, there was a cacophony emanating from the street below. From the American saloons he could hear two pianos competing. The one that was most off-key seemed to be winning the battle. From the Mexican end of town, he heard the strumming of a guitar and the high, plaintive wail of a trumpet. The voices of scores of animated conversations spilled out through the open windows and doors of the town's buildings, and somewhere someone was singing. He heard a gunshot but knew instinctively that it was not a shot fired in anger. That was borne out by the fact that the shot was followed by a woman's high-pitched scream, then a man's deep-voiced laughter.

Lucas blew out his lantern and, disregarding the sign on the wall, went to bed fully dressed, without removing his boots or his spurs.

11

The dream returned. It didn't occur as often as it once did, but when it did occur it was as frightening and dominating as it ever was, and he was unable to separate the dream of Andersonville with the actuality of the infamous Confederate prison of war camp where Lucas spent the last year of the civil war.

Lucas Cain found himself in a dream, transported back to the haunting memories of his past. But he could not differentiate the memories from the actual events. He wasn't dreaming, he was there.

The air was thick with tension as he stood in the desolate grounds of Andersonville Prison, the place that had once confined him, did so again in a living nightmare. The wooden palisade loomed high above, casting long shadows over the weary faces of the prisoners.

As he walked through the compound, the distant moans of the suffering echoed in his ears. Lucas could feel the weight of hunger, the sting of despair, and the palpable fear that gripped every soul in this accursed place. Faces of fellow captives flashed before his eyes, each one etched with the pain of captivity.

Suddenly, the scene shifted. Lucas found himself aboard the ill-fated Sultana, the riverboat that had promised freedom but delivered tragedy. The air was thick with smoke and the distant cries of men struggling against the currents. The boat trembled as it battled the mighty Mississippi, burdened with the weight of those seeking home.

Lucas stood on the deck, watching as the river swallowed the vessel whole. The water churned with chaos, and the screams of the doomed echoed in the night. Panic set in, and Lucas felt the icy grip of the river pulling him under.

Then, in the dream, Lucas was underwater, surrounded by swirling darkness. It felt like an eternity, struggling against the currents, his chest tightening with the desperate need for air. Just when it seemed he would succumb to the depths, a shimmering light appeared, pulling him upward.

Gasping for air, Lucas broke the surface and found himself on the riverbank, battered but alive. The dream brought a flood of emotions—the relief of survival mixed with the heavy burden of loss for those who hadn't made it.

As he stood on the riverbank, the dream shifted once more. Lucas found himself in a quiet, sunlit meadow. The air was crisp, and the scent of wildflowers surrounded him. In the distance, he saw the faces of those he had lost—comrades from Andersonville and fellow passengers from the Sultana. They smiled, nodding in silent acknowledgment.

Lucas felt a sense of closure, a bittersweet peace settling over him. The dream was a tapestry of his past, woven with the threads of pain, resilience, and the indomitable spirit that had carried him through the darkest moments of his life.

As the dream faded, Lucas Cain awoke, finding himself not in Andersonville, or struggling for his life, but lying in the bed he had rented for the night. The memories lingered, but so did the newfound sense of peace. The echoes of Andersonville and the Sultana would forever be a part of him, but in the light of dawn, he faced a new day with the strength born from surviving the crucible of war.

Beside the bed, a slight morning breeze filled the muslin curtains and lifted them out over the wide-planked floor. Lucas moved to the window and looked out over the town, which was just beginning to awaken. Water was being heated behind the laundry and boxes were being stacked behind the grocery store. A team of four big horses pulled a fully loaded freight wagon down the main street.

From somewhere Lucas could smell bacon frying and his stomach growled, reminding him that he was hungry. He splashed some water in the basin, washed his face and hands, then put on his hat and went downstairs for breakfast.

Half an hour later Lucas was enjoying a breakfast of bacon, eggs, and fried potatoes when a boy of about sixteen came over to his table.

"Excuse me, sir," the boy said. "Are you Lucas Cain?"

"Yeah," Lucas said.

"My name is Billy Williams, Mr. Cain. I have your horse outside."

"My horse? I don't have a horse."

"You do now," Billy said. He smiled broadly. "You've got the best horse in town. You want to see it?"

Lucas put on his hat, got up from the table, and followed Billy outside. Standing at the hitching rail was as fine a looking example of horseflesh as he had ever seen. He noticed also, that it was already saddled, with his saddle.

"Where'd this horse come from?" Lucas asked.

"From Crawford's," Billy said.

"Crawford?"

"He owns the livery stable. It's about the only place left in town that ain't owned by Jules Tudway. I work for Mr. Crawford."

"That doesn't explain how I got the horse."

"Well, sir, some old man in funny-looking clothes and with a funny accent come into the stable this morning and bought him," the boy said. "'I would like to purchase a horse,' he said. That was the word he used. Purchase. 'And I want the best animal you have,' he said. I told him this one was the best we had, but he was three hundred dollars. Well sir, that fella never blinked an eye. 'I'll take it,' he said. Then he said 'Please see to it that Mr. Lucas Cain takes delivery of the animal.' And that's what I'm doin' here," Billy concluded. "I'm seein' to it that you take delivery."

"How did my saddle get on him?" Lucas asked.

The boy smiled. "Heck, mister, you're Lucas Cain. You think I don't know who you are? The whole town knows who you are and what you done on the train yesterday. I know'd you'd checked your saddle down to the depot, so I just went down there, got it, and put it on your horse for you."

"Thanks," Lucas said.

"Say, mister?" Billy asked. "Iffen it was to come down to it, do you think you could take Deke Pauley?"

"I don't know," Lucas said. "I've never had to try him."

"Well, I know that," Billy said. "If you had, one of you would be dead. But the question I'm askin' is, which one?"

"The one that loses," Lucas replied.

"Well, I wouldn't mind seein' Pauley lose, that's for sure."

"You don't like Mr. Pauley?"

"Don't know that much about him," Billy said. "But I hear that he's started workin' for Tudway, and since I don't like Tudway, I just naturally don't like anyone who works for him."

"I thought Tudway was the big man in these parts," Lucas said. "I thought he was everyone's friend."

"Not everyone's friend," Billy answered. "You know, Mr. Cain, I didn't always work in a stable. Time was when my ma and pa and me run a ranch. It wasn't a very big ranch, but since Pa and me didn't have no hands, it was just the right size for us to run alone. But that's all gone now. Tudway stole the ranch from us. My pa, he got so upset he died of the apoplexy. My ma died of a heart that was pure-dee broke. No, sir, Jules Tudway ain't no friend of mine. So if you ever do go up against Pauley, I hope I'm around to watch. And when it's over, I hope you're the one still standin'. Be seein' you again sometime," he concluded with a wave. Then he started back down the street toward Crawford's Livery Stable.

Lucas knew that the horse had come from Mrs. Davenport and he didn't feel quite right, taking it.

"I'll tell you this, though," he said, talking to the horse. "You're about as fine a looking horse as I've seen. Let's go see Mrs. Davenport."

After breakfast in the Chuckwagon Café, Lucas rode over to the sheriff's office, then went inside to see if he had any money coming from the four men he had brought in last night.

"None," the sheriff said.

"You checked the capital?"

"I checked."

"What about up in Colorado? Kansas? Over in New Mexico? Did you check there?"

"No, and I didn't check China either," the sheriff answered. "I told you, Cain, there ain't no dodgers out on these men. These men worked for Mr. Tudway. As a matter of fact, if I were you, I'd be leavin' town about now. Mr. Tudway don't take too kindly to people killing his men."

"And does that include you, Sheriff Slater? Are you one of Tudway's men?" Lucas asked.

"Bought and paid for," a woman's voice said and Lucas turned to see Mrs. Davenport and Malcolm standing in the front door.

"See here, Mrs. Davenport," Slater said. "You got no right to say something like that."

"Oh, don't I?" Mrs. Davenport said. "I have every right. I have sent you two letters and a telegram asking for some action. And what have you done? Nothing."

"Being reasonable, Mrs. Davenport," the sheriff said. "You got no proof. I'm not going to go charging out to Winning Hand with no proof."

Mrs. Davenport laughed a short, derisive laugh. "Sheriff Slater, you wouldn't charge into Winning Hand with all the proof in the world and with the United States Army marching along beside you. Come along, Malcolm. We're wasting our time here."

Mrs. Davenport turned away angrily, then swept back down the street toward her private car. The sheriff stood in the window, watching her for a moment, then he turned back to Lucas.

"Who the hell does she think she is?" the sheriff asked. "Ridin' around in that fancy railcar, tryin' to tell me how to do my job. She's tryin' to fool people into thinkin' she's some great lady, or somethin'. Well, I could tell you a few stories about her if you'd like to know."

"I don't want to hear any of them," Lucas said. "The lady is my friend."

"Your friend, huh? Well, it's too bad you didn't run into her some years back. From what I hear she was *real* friendly with men then. They say there was a time when...aghhh!" The sheriff's tale was interrupted by the barrel of a pistol, shoved into his throat. His eyes grew wide with fright and he looked at Lucas in terror and confusion.

"I said I didn't want to hear any of the stories," Lucas said quietly. "Do I make myself clear now?"

To the degree that the sheriff could respond with the pistol barrel shoved halfway down his throat, he nodded yes. Lucas took the gun out of the sheriff's mouth, wiped the barrel on the sheriff's pant leg, then put it away.

"What's the matter with you? Are you crazy?" the sheriff asked.

"Just crazy enough to give me an edge," Lucas said. He twisted his mouth into what might have been a smile. "This way nobody ever knows just what I'm going to do."

"Somebody could get hurt, you doin' something like that," the sheriff said, taking his handkerchief out to wipe his mouth. The blade sight of Lucas's pistol had cut his lip and he pulled the handkerchief away to examine the blood. There wasn't much.

"Generally, somebody does get hurt," Lucas replied easily. "Lots of times they get killed. Only it isn't me."

After Lucas left the sheriff's office, he got a bath and a haircut at the barbershop, then changed into his clean shirt and pants while he took the ones he was wearing to the laundry. He bought some fresh bullets for his gun, then some coffee, beans, and jerky. He waited until his laundry was done, then picked it up and started to ride out of town. With Press Gibson already dead, there was nothing to keep him here. Even if there was anyone with the price on their head, it would be slim pickings, hardly worth hanging around for.

DEKE PAULEY HAD GIVEN up being a bounty hunter when he took the job of head of protection for Jules Tudway. The salary Tudway offered was exceptionally good, and Pauley knew that it would be more dependable than bounty hunting. It was also less stressful, though from what he had already learned, he knew it would have its dangerous moments.

"So you've give up bein' a bounty hunter?" Sheriff Slater asked.

"Well, to the degree that I can, now that I'm working for Mr. Tudway, I want to keep my hand in the game, but it's not something I want to do all the time now," Pauley said. "At least, not like my friend, Lucas Cain."

"That's right, you and Cain are friends, ain't you?"

"That we are."

"I have to tell you, Mr. Pauley, I don't care much for your choice of friends."

"I don't remember asking you whether you cared or not," Pauley said in a tone of voice that Sheriff Slater found frightening.

12

On the way out of town, Lucas stopped at the sidetrack, tied off his horse, then climbed up onto the vestibule of Mrs. Davenport's private car and knocked on the door. Malcolm answered it.

"Good afternoon, sir," Malcolm said. He stepped away from the door. "Won't you please come in?"

"Yes, thank you," Lucas said, taking off his hat as he stepped inside.

"Mr. Cain," Mrs. Davenport said, greeting him. "I do hope you haven't had your lunch. Malcolm has prepared a delightful meal for us."

"For us? You mean you were expecting me?"

"Yes. I figured you would stop by before you left to thank me for the horse," Mrs. Davenport said. She fixed him with a hard gaze. "You *are* going to thank me for him, aren't you?"

"Yeah," Lucas said. "Yeah, that's why I'm here. But I didn't know I was going to eat."

"Well, now you know. Is it a good horse?"

"It's a very good horse."

"What did you name him?"

"Charley Three," Lucas said.

"Charley Three? I hope you don't mind my saying so, but that's a strange name for a horse. Why did you choose that name?"

"I've had Charley One, and Charley Two. They were both good horses, and Charley Three will be honored to be named after them."

Mrs. Davenport laughed heartily. "How like you, Lucas Cain. You are a practical man who lets nothing get in the way of what you go after."

"I try not to."

"Sit. Eat," Mrs. Davenport invited.

The meal was some sort of veal with a white wine sauce. Lucas had never tasted anything like it before and he thought it was delicious. When Malcolm offered to fill Lucas plate a second time, he gladly accepted.

"Let's talk a little business, Lucas Cain," Mrs. Davenport said as Lucas began his second serving.

"What kind of business?"

"You are a bounty hunter, right?"

"I prefer to think of myself as a US Marshal, but, yes, I hunt people down and turn them in for bounties."

"You wanted to collect for those men you killed last night, but unless I miss my guess, there was no bounty. And on top of that, I understand that the man you had wanted to hunt down was killed by someone else, so you lost the bounty on him as well."

"You're right again," Lucas said.

"How much bounty did you lose? What was the reward?"

"Fifteen hundred dollars," Lucas said.

"Fifteen hundred," Mrs. Davenport repeated. "Suppose I told you about a bounty of ten thousand dollars? Would you be interested?"

"Ten thousand dollars? I don't know of anyone who has a bounty of ten thousand dollars," Lucas said.

"I know someone who has a bounty of ten thousand dollars," Mrs. Davenport said. "His name is Roberto Ortiz."

"I've never heard of him," Lucas admitted. "That's a Mexican name. Is that ten thousand dollars American?"

"You've never heard of him, because he is only five years old," Mrs. Davenport said. "And yes, it is ten thousand dollars American, because *I'm* the one who will be paying the bounty to anyone who will find him. Now, how about it, Mr. Cain? Are you interested?"

"For ten thousand dollars? Oh yes, ma'am, I'm interested, all right," Lucas said. He took a drink of his wine. Like the sipping whiskey the night before, it was very good. "Who is this Roberto Ortiz and why are you willing to pay ten thousand dollars for him?"

"He is a poor, motherless boy," Mrs. Davenport said. "The son of Carlos Ortiz, my foreman at Davenport Court. Roberto was kidnapped by Jules Tudway."

"That's what you were talking to the sheriff about, isn't it?"

"Yes," Mrs. Davenport said. "The sheriff says he won't act because I have no proof. The sheriff won't act because he's either Tudway's man, or he's too frightened to go against him. Down here, everyone is. But the sheriff is right about one thing. I have no proof. That's why I haven't been able to get help from anyone else, either."

"If you have no proof, how do you know Tudway has the boy?"

"I know he has the boy," Mrs. Davenport said. "If you need proof, I'm sorry, I can't furnish that."

Lucas laughed. "Mrs. Davenport, I don't try people in a court of law. To my way of looking at things, there are only two sides to the coin. True or not true. If it is true that Tudway has the boy, then I don't give a damn about having the proof."

Mrs. Davenport smiled broadly. "I knew we were going to be able to work together," she said. She got up from the dining table and stepped over to a trunk. She opened it, foraged around a bit, then came back to the table with a handful of documents.

"First, I want you to look at this." She spread out one of the rolls of paper and held the edges down with silverware from the table. Lucas saw that it was a map.

"Here is Davenport Court, up here." She pointed to a sizable piece of land. "This is Tudway's ranch, Winning Hand." Lucas could see that Winning Hand was a much larger piece. "As you can see, for several miles, the borders of the two ranches are contiguous. But these," she continued, "are the ranches that are causing all the trouble." There were a half-dozen smaller spreads wedged in between Winning Hand and Davenport Court.

"Trouble?"

"Well, not for me," Mrs. Davenport explained. "For Tudway. He has already bought or run out all the people who were working these ranches." As Mrs. Davenport spoke, Lucas could tell that several pieces of land had been consolidated into Winning Hand. "He didn't have much trouble doing that because he controlled their water. The Diablo River runs across his property, and as you can see on the map here, it also feeds these ranches down here. But the map is deceiving, Mr. Cain. There is no Diablo River anymore, at least not beyond this point. Jules Tudway has completely stopped its flow. But now look at these ranches, the ones that are still operating."

Lucas examined them, then found a creek that flowed through each of them. He followed the creek back to its source.

"The springhead is on your land," he said.

"Yes. And as long as I control that springhead the smaller ranchers are assured of their fair share. If Tudway ever once gets his hands on the springhead, then he will do with it exactly as he did with the Diablo. Once the water is gone, these smaller ranchers will be gone, and once they're gone, *I'll* be the little rancher and he'll come after me."

"Is it true that Winning Hand was once a part of Davenport Court?"

"This part of it was," Mrs. Davenport admitted, running her hand across a sizable portion of the land. "Of course, he's enlarged it considerably by his ruthless takeover of the smaller ranchers."

"Why did you sell it to him?"

"It wasn't me, it was Mr. Davenport before we were even married. And he didn't exactly *sell* the land to him."

"What do you mean, he didn't exactly sell it? How did Tudway get it?"

Mrs. Davenport sighed. "My husband was a wonderful man, Mr. Cain. But he had one vice, one terrible vice. He liked to gamble. He got into a card game with Tudway, and before I could stop him, he had already lost more than half his land. Fortunately, he managed to hold on to the springhead and it's that springhead that is providing the water the smaller ranchers need. And it's that springhead that Tudway is after now. He's trying to force me to sell it to him."

"Don't sell it," Lucas said.

"It isn't quite that simple," Mrs. Davenport said. She put down another piece of paper. "Here is a letter from Tudway. And in it, he offers to help locate and return the boy safely, if I will agree to sell him the springhead."

Lucas looked at the letter. "He doesn't say he has the boy."

"He doesn't *have* to say that," Mrs. Davenport said. "He has the boy. Believe me."

Lucas was quiet for a moment as he examined the map. "I believe you," he finally said.

"Then you'll help?"

"Mrs. Davenport, have you ever heard of me?" Lucas asked.

"Yes. I've heard of you," she said.

"What have you heard?"

"I've heard that you are a Deputy US Marshal who has some arrangement that allows you to collect bounties."

"What else have you heard?"

"Shall I be frank, Mr. Cain? I have heard that people have a habit of getting killed around you," she said.

"That's true, people do have a habit of dying around me," Lucas said. "I guess you saw an example of it last night. I didn't set out to kill those men, but somehow it all seems to build upon itself. When people are around me, they try to kill me and I have no choice. I generally have to kill them."

"So what are you telling me, Mr. Cain?"

"I'm telling you that if I go onto Winning Hand Ranch to look for Roberto, some people are going to be killed. Maybe a lot of people. Does that bother you?"

"Not if you get the job done," Mrs. Davenport replied.

"Why is this boy so important to you?"

"I told you, he's my foreman's son," Mrs. Davenport said. "He wouldn't even be in danger if it weren't for me. Tudway is using an innocent boy to force me to sell him that springhead. I feel responsible for that."

"And that's all?"

Mrs. Davenport studied Lucas for a long moment, then she sighed. "Not quite," she said. "I told you that Roberto was a poor, motherless child. The boy's mother died in childbirth. The boy's mother was like my own daughter. One of the girls in the saloon where I worked had her, then abandoned her. I brought her with me from San Francisco, and I raised her as my own. You can see, then, that the boy means a great deal to me."

"Did Tudway know about your relationship with the boy's mother?" Lucas asked.

"Oh yes, he knew," Mrs. Davenport said. "He was there."

"I beg your pardon?"

"Tudway was there. He was in San Francisco. Mr. Cain, I told you that Tudway won Winning Hand from my husband in a card game. What I didn't tell you was *where* that card game took place."

"San Francisco?" Lucas asked.

"Yes. Jules Tudway was a gambler in the same saloon where I worked. That was where and when I met Mr. Davenport. He had already lost half his ranch when I saw what was going on. I convinced Rowland to stop playing before he lost everything." She smiled. "I could be pretty convincing in those days."

"Was Tudway cheating?"

"I honestly don't know," Mrs. Davenport replied. "There may have been no need to cheat. My husband was a terrible gambler. Tudway, on the other hand, is very good at it. He's also cool under fire, Mr. Cain. If you take on this job, I have to warn you, he's a dangerous character who plays for very high stakes."

Lucas drummed his fingers on the table and looked at Mrs. Davenport.

"There's one more thing you need to know," Mrs. Davenport said.

"What's that?"

"Deke Pauley now works for Jules Tudway."

"Billy Williams mentioned that when he brought me the horse."

"He's your friend, isn't he?"

"Yes, I would say that," Lucas said. "We were partners for a while."

"Will it bother you if you have to cross Pauley?" Mrs. Davenport asked. "When Tudway finds out you're working for me, he may try to play on your friendship. I'll say this about Tudway. He's a very high-stakes player."

"I'll tell you what," Lucas said. "Ten thousand dollars makes me a high-stakes player too. I think I'll just sit in on this game."

As Deke Pauley surveyed the vast expanse of the ranch he now served, he couldn't shake the unease settling in his gut. The ruthless ranch owner, Jules Tudway, had promised him wealth and power, but Pauley knew that such promises often came at a steep price.

Lucas Cain, his one-time partner and friend, was a name etched in Pauley's mind. He unconsciously began to rub his leg. Had it not been for Lucas, Deke knew he would be dead. Had he not gotten him to San Martin and to the doctor, gangrene would have, at the very least, taken his leg. Those memories were now tainted by the choice Pauley had made. The job offer Tudway had proposed had been too tempting, the allure of wealth too strong to resist. But with each passing day, he found himself haunted by a sense of betrayal.

The ranch owner's private army, which Pauley now led, was a force to be reckoned with. His every order was met with unquestioning obedience, and the men under his command were as loyal as they were formidable. Yet, for all the power he wielded, Pauley couldn't escape the feeling that he was walking a treacherous path.

Like Deke, Lucas Cain was a skilled tracker and a sharpshooter. The two had relied on each other's instincts and skills to bring men to justice back when justice was a coin toss away. But now he knew he and Lucas were on opposite sides. He understood that Lucas was still seeking justice for the common man, while he was enforcing the will of a man whose ethics even Deke could see were shady.

The subject of Pauley's contemplation was at the time visiting with Mrs. Davenport.

"The first thing I'm going to do is talk to Tudway and ask him about the child," Lucas said as he was finishing his lunch with Mrs. Davenport.

"How are you going to even get in to see him?" Mrs. Davenport asked.

"I'm going to take something back to him that belongs to him."

"What will you be taking to him?"

"It's really more of a question of who I'll be taking to him, rather than what I'll be taking," Lucas replied.

"WHAT THE HELL do you mean you want the four bodies you brought in?" Sheriff Slater asked. "Do you think I just keep them around? They're with the undertaker."

"He hasn't buried them yet, has he?"

"No, he's waiting for the money from the county."

"Well, in that case, he and the county both should be happy to get rid of them."

"I don't know what the hell you want with 'em, but as far as I'm concerned you can have 'em," Slater said.

ABOUT AN HOUR AND A HALF LATER, Lucas looked back over his shoulder as he led the four horses across the swiftly running stream. Each animal was carrying a body, belly down, across its back. The bodies were each wrapped in a tarpaulin, but that didn't keep the horses from smelling death, and they didn't like it one little bit.

The horses were the same ones the men had been riding when they stopped the train. A freight train crew found the horses the next day, calmly cropping grass alongside the track right where the outlaws had left them. They put the horses in an empty cattle car and brought them on into Tudway.

Lucas didn't know which body belonged to which horse. He just tossed them on, first served. The sheriff told him he was a fool to be taking the bodies out to Winning Hand, but he didn't do anything to stop him.

The horses kicked up sheets of silver spray as they trotted through the stream. Lucas would have paused to give them an opportunity to drink if they wanted to, but none of them did. It was as if they were anxious to get to where they were going so they could rid themselves of their gruesome cargo.

Once across the stream, Lucas turned back around to pay attention to where he was going. For some time now he had been aware that two men were dogging him, riding parallel with him and, for the most part, staying out of sight. He was pretty sure they were Winning Hand men, and they were good at what they were doing. They were good, but Lucas was better. He had picked them up the moment they started shadowing him.

Lucas rode on for a couple more miles, all the while keeping his eye on them, until finally he decided to do something about it. He waited until the trail led in between two parallel rows of hills. Once into the defile, he dropped the line to the lead horse, knowing that it could only go forward, then cut off the trail and, using the ridge line to conceal his movement, rode ahead about two hundred yards. He went over to the gulley his two tails were using, dismounted, then pulled his rifle from the saddle scabbard and climbed onto a rocky ledge to wait for them. He jacked a round into the chamber.

Lucas watched and waited. He saw them come around a bend in the gulley and knew that not only had they not seen him, they hadn't even missed him. When they were right on him, he suddenly stood up.

"Hold it!" he shouted.

"Damn," one of the riders yelled. He had to fight to stay on his horse, for the horse had been so startled that it reared. The other rider started for his gun.

"Don't do it!" Lucas said, raising his rifle to his shoulder.

"Gus! Keep your hand away from your gun!" the first rider said, just now regaining control of his horse.

"You'd better listen to your friend," Lucas said.

Gus stopped his draw. "Where'd you come from?" he asked.

"You ought to know," Lucas replied. "You've been dogging my tail for the last five miles."

"I don't know what you're talking about."

"Mister, don't insult my intelligence," Lucas said. "That makes me mad."

"All right, we been dogging you," the first rider admitted.

"What do you want?"

"You're on Winning Hand land."

"From what I hear, I could ride for two or three days and still be on Winning Hand land," Lucas said.

"That's about the size of it," the first rider said. "What are you doing here?"

"I'm paying a friendly visit."

"We're not friendly and we don't like visitors," Gus said. "Mister, you'd be a hell of a lot better off if you'd just turn around and go back to where you came from."

"That's not the way it works," Lucas said. "I am the one holding the gun here. I'm the one who gives the orders." He motioned toward the draw with the barrel of his rifle. "I have four pack horses I've been leading, and they will be coming out of there directly. How about you fellas picking them up and leading them on into the main house?"

"What are you packing on those animals?"

"Something that belongs to Winning Hand," Lucas said.

The first of the four horses appeared then, and Gus looked over toward them.

"Damn! Ray, look at that! Them horses belong to Tim, Johnny, Ira, and Carter. He's packin' 'em in."

"Mister, you want to tell me what happened to them boys?" Ray asked.

"I killed them," Lucas said.

"You killed 'em? All four of 'em?"

"All four of them."

"There's no way you could've got all four of 'em without shootin' 'em in the back."

"The holes are in front," Lucas said easily.

"You killed 'em and you're bringin' 'em in?"

"That's right."

"All I can say about you, mister, is you must be tired of livin'," Ray said.

"You lead the way in," Lucas said.

Grumbling, the two cowboys took two horses each and started riding.

It took two more hours of steady riding before they reached their destination. There at the spigot, Lucas saw a young, very pretty Mexican woman filling a bucket with water. A couple of geese, several chickens, and a handful of guinea hens honked, squawked, and flapped their wings to get out of the way as the little party road across the wide plaza. A dog, attracted by the scent, ran alongside the four horses, yapping at the canvas bundles that were draped across the saddles.

When they drew even with the water tank, Lucas dismounted. He touched the brim of his hat to the young señorita at the spigot. She filled her bucket and turned off the spigot, acknowledged his greeting with a pretty, but embarrassed, smile, then tossing one last look over her shoulder, hurried back to the main house. Lucas took down the dipper, filled it and began drinking, allowing the water to cascade down his mouth to his shirt. As he was drinking a man came out of the main house. The man spoke to the two cowboys Lucas had herded in, then he went over and pulled the canvas aside to look at one of the bodies. With the canvas opened, the smell hit him hard and Lucas saw him jerk his head back quickly then put a handkerchief to his nose. He made an impatient motion with the back of his hand, said something Lucas was too far away to hear, and the two riders took the four bodies away. The man started toward the water tank.

Lucas took his canteen down from his saddle and held it under the spigot. He watched as a man approached him. He already knew that Deke Pauley was working for Jules Tudway, but this was the first time he had seen visible proof.

When Pauley and Lucas had parted it had been amicable enough, and in a world of very few friends, Lucas would have counted Pauley as one of them.

Pauley smiled broadly as he approached. "Well, I'll be damned. If it ain't Lucas Cain. You're sure a sight for sore eyes," he said.

"Hello, Deke," Lucas said "I hear you had a little shoot-out with Press Gibson the other day. Have you put in for your reward? There was fifteen hundred on him."

"It was up to two thousand," Deke said. "Well, I guess I was kind of lucky, him just fallin' into my lap like that. Then, of course, I don't guess he actually just fell in, did he? What with you chasing him."

"No, it was your luck. It took a while to track down John Babcock and I was just starting after Gibson," Lucas said.

"Well, that's the way things happen, sometimes chicken, sometimes feathers," Deke said. "Tell me have you been back to Eastland to see Carolina?"

"No."

"You're a fool, Lucas. She was one, good-looking woman. A good woman too, and smart as a tack."

"She is, indeed," Lucas said.

"Well, it's good to see you, Lucas. Damn good," Pauley said. He jerked his head toward the four horses, which were now over by the barn. A couple of men were off-loading the bodies. "Them boys is pretty ripe."

"Got a right to be. They been dead a couple of days now," Lucas answered.

"Who killed them?"

"I did."

"Yeah, that's sort of what I thought. You want to tell me what happened?"

"They stopped the train," Lucas said. "I was on the train, minding my own business, Next thing I knew, I was right in the middle of a gunfight."

"Well, that bein' the case, I reckon there wasn't much you could do about it," Pauley said.

"Not if I wanted to stay alive."

"That's what I figured. Tell you what. I'll see what I can do toward makin' Mr. Tudway understand it like that," Pauley said. "The only thing is, he takes it real personal whenever somethin' happens to one of his riders. Don't mind tellin' you, though, that's goin' to take some doin'. For some reason he was particular partial toward Tim Barnet."

"Where do you fit in here, Deke? I mean, I heard you were workin' for Tudway, but what exactly do you do?"

Deke smiled. "Oh, Lucas, I'm fixed up real good here. Fact is, I couldn't ask for a better situation. I'm Mr. Tudway's ramrod," he said.

"Deke Pauley ramroding a ranch? Never thought I'd see that happen."

"I know. Ain't this the beatin'est thing, though?"

Pauley said. "But the pay is real good and it ain't like I'm actual punchin' cows. I mean, hell, I don't hardly ever see a cow."

"How the hell can you ramrod a ranch without seeing a cow?"

"We got other folks to take care of that," Deke said. "I take care of ever'thing else."

Lucas finished filling his canteen, then he corked it and hooked it back on the pommel. "Uh-huh," he said. "And what would everything else be?"

"A man like Mr. Tudway has lots of enemies," Deke said.

"And that's your job, is it? To take care of his enemies for him?"

Deke smiled. "Yep. You might say I'm still in the same line of work I always was. I'm still gettin' paid for my guns, only I'm gettin' paid a lot more than you usually find on a dodger and I don't have to haul some stinkin' carcass into the sheriff's office to pick up my money. Except for that business with Gibson, and like I say, he just sort of fell into my lap."

"Sounds like you have a good deal here," Lucas said.

"I do. Say, would you like to meet Mr. Tudway?" Deke invited. "I bet you could work out the same kind of a deal with him."

"You mean I could work for Tudway?"

"Sure you could. If I put in a good word for you."

Lucas chuckled. "Everyone else has been telling me that I was going to get myself killed by riding in here like this. But here you're tellin' me I can get hired."

"Well, the truth is, if anybody else had brought those bodies in, they probably would be dead by now," Deke said. "But you got a friend in court, you might say."

"You?"

"Me," Deke said, smiling broadly and pointing to his chest with his thumb. "Come on into the big house. I want you to meet Mr. Tudway."

"Don't mind if I do," Lucas replied. He followed Pauley across a stone patio, under a series of adobe arches, then down a long walkway flanked by beds of bright red geraniums. Inside the house the parlor was dark and cooled by half a dozen hanging pots of water, a trick the Southwest settlers had learned from the Indians.

"Wait here," Deke said. "I have some business to tend to, but Mr. Tudway will be here in a couple of minutes."

"Thanks," Lucas said.

"It was really good seein' you again, Lucas," Deke said as he left the room.

During the few moments Lucas was alone, he looked around. At the back of the room was a stairway leading up to the second floor. From where he was standing, he could see as far up the stairs as the first landing, but from there, the stairs made a sharp turn to the right and he could see no more of it. He turned his attention to the room itself. A large painting was hanging by wires over a cold fireplace. The painting was of a rather noble-looking figure wearing a colonel's uniform and sitting astride a white horse. The military officer in the picture was white-haired and blue-eyed. Lucas walked over to examine the painting more closely. He sensed rather than heard someone come into the room behind him and turned to see, in the flesh, the man he had just been looking at in the portrait. Lucas looked from the man to the painting.

"Oh yes, I'll admit that there is a bit of grandiose pretentiousness in that picture," the man said with a little chuckle. "I mean, to portray myself in uniform suggests that I may have led troops in battle when the truth of the matter is, I have never even been in battle. I'm afraid I am a colonel in name only. The military governor appointed me a colonel in the territorial militia, but the rank is strictly honorary. Mr. Cain, I am Jules Tudway."

"Mr. Tudway," Lucas said. Tudway didn't cross the room to offer his hand, and neither did Lucas.

"Pauley told me what happened to Tim and the others. I can't imagine what got into them," Tudway said. "It just doesn't seem like them to try and rob a train like that."

"They weren't trying to rob the train."

"They weren't? But isn't that what you told Pauley?"

"I told Pauley they *stopped* a train, not that they were trying to rob it. What they had in mind was to kidnap Mrs. Davenport," Lucas said. "What were they going to do with her, Tudway? Were they going to bring her here?"

Tudway went over to a highly polished table and opened a silver case from which he extracted a long, thin cheroot. He struck a match, held it to the end of the cheroot, and puffed until his head was wreathed in tobacco smoke. He studied Lucas through narrowed eyes for a long moment before he spoke.

"Yes," he said. "I wanted to bring her here. You see, Mr. Cain, I've been trying to get her to come see me on her own, but she won't do it. And that's too bad because we have a lot of important things to take care of, things like water and grazing rights, land disposition, and our standin' together against homesteaders and poachers. I mean, it's only right that she and I, as the two biggest landowners in the territory, come to some accord. But Mrs. Davenport doesn't see it as I do. She lets old wounds stand in the way."

"So, since she wouldn't meet with you, you decided to send your men to bring her back as your prisoner," Lucas said. "Is that it?"

"Yes. I didn't intend to hurt her, you understand. In fact, I didn't want anyone to get hurt, and I thought this was the only way. But I understand the lady, Cain," Tudway said. "I underestimated her and it cost me the lives of four of my best men. I had no idea she would hire you to ride on that train with her."

"I wasn't working for her," Lucas said. "What I told Pauley was the truth. Your men started shooting at me, and I had no choice. I had to shoot back."

"Yes, so I understand. But let me tell you why I'm having trouble with that. They were good men, you see," Tudway said. "All four of them were crack shots, and it's hard to believe that they could have the drop on you, four to one, and yet when the shootin' started, you would come out on top."

"That shouldn't be so hard to believe. I've seen better men and longer odds," Lucas said easily. "And so has Pauley."

"Yes, I'm quite pleased with Pauley's work. And he tells me that you might be interested in working for me."

"That was Pauley's idea," Lucas replied. "Not mine. I can't work for you. I've already got a job."

"Doing what? Running down highwaymen and store robbers for a few hundred dollars? From what I hear, you came up empty with Press Gibson."

"I'm working for Mrs. Davenport."

Tudway pulled the cheroot away from his mouth in surprise. "Wait a minute. I thought you said you *weren't* working for her."

"I said I wasn't working for her when I killed your

men," Lucas said. "But all that has changed. I *am* working for her *now*."

"I see. That's very interesting. Tell me, Cain, just what is it you are supposed to be doing for her?"

"Mrs. Davenport hired me to find Roberto Ortiz and bring him home."

Though the cheroot was only smoked halfway down, Tudway walked over to an ashtray that was as silver as the case the cheroot had come from and grounded it out.

"Yes, I know how upset she must be that the boy is gone," he said. "I myself offered to help find him and bring him back."

"In return for the deed to the springhead?" Lucas asked.

"I won't lie to you," Tudway said. "If I'm going to turn loose the biggest army of men this side of Fort Riley, Kansas, just to look for one small boy, I expect to be adequately compensated for it. It seemed like a fair bargain to me. I mean, considering who the boy is and all."

"You mean her foreman's son," Lucas said.

Tudway stuck the cheroot in his mouth and smiled. "I'll be damned. You don't know, do you?" he said.

"Know what?"

"The boy is Mrs. Davenport's grandson."

13

"You didn't tell me the boy was your grandchild," Lucas accused. He and Mrs. Davenport were in her private railway car on the siding at Tudway.

Mrs. Davenport leaned back in her chair and put her hands together in front of her face, fingertip to fingertip.

"Jules Tudway told you that, did he?"

"Yes. Is it true?"

"I imagine he took a great deal of pleasure in revealing my sordid past to you. Yes, the boy's mother was my daughter."

"Did your husband know?"

"He knew," Mrs. Davenport said. "He said it didn't bother him. He just wasn't sure if his friends and neighbors would understand his marrying someone who was not only a saloon girl but was bringing along an illegitimate child in the bargain."

"What about the boy?" Lucas asked. "Does Roberto know?"

"No, he doesn't," Mrs. Davenport said. "Oh, he'll be told someday. But for now, both his father and I thought it best that he not know. Mr. Cain, I'm sorry I wasn't entirely truthful with you," she apologized. "The story I told you is the story my husband wanted me to tell our friends. I guess it became a habit with me. Anyway, does it really make a difference?"

"I reckon not," Lucas said. "Except that I don't like surprises. Surprises give the other man the advantage."

"I can understand that," Mrs. Davenport said. "All right, no more surprises."

Half an hour after this conversation, Lucas was sitting at a table in the corner of the Golden Eagle Saloon, eating a supper of bacon and beans. He knew Mrs. Davenport had planned for him to take supper with her, because even as they were talking, he had noticed Malcolm scurrying about the kitchen of the private car preparing one of his specialties. But Lucas left before the invitation could be issued. It wasn't because he liked bacon and beans better than the fancy fare prepared by Malcolm or that he enjoyed the company of town drunks, smelly cowhands, and painted doxies to that of Mrs. Davenport's. He left because intuitively he knew that such soft living could take away his edge.

A bar girl sidled over to his table and stood there for a moment, smiling down at him, hoping to be invited to join him. The girl was young, probably barely into her twenties, and yet her life "on the line" was already beginning to take its toll in dissipation. Though she was smiling, the smile didn't quite reach her eyes. And those same eyes were tired, frightened, and dispirited. Her hair was long and light brown, her dispirited eyes were blue.

Lucas kicked out a chair with his foot, inviting the girl to join him.

"Thanks," she said. She nodded at the bartender, who

appeared as if by magic to pour her a drink. "My name is Sally."

All the girls in the bar drank from a special bottle of whiskey, weakened with water so that it barely had the color and smell of the real thing. There were two reasons for this. One was that by keeping the liquor so weak, the girls could drink all night long without getting drunk. The other was that there was so little whiskey in one of the girls' drinks that each one sold was almost a hundred percent profit for the saloon. It was in this way that the saloon could afford to give the girls one-half of what they sold. Some of the patrons resented paying full price for diluted whiskey, but it didn't bother Lucas so long as he wasn't having to drink it.

"I know who you are," Sally said. "You're the man who slept here the other night. Alone."

"Yes."

"What a shame," she teased. "I mean, you all alone in that great big bed. Why, the thought of it just broke my heart."

"You seemed busy enough," Lucas said. He remembered seeing her go up the stairs with a cowboy just before he went up.

"You noticed me? I'm flattered," Sally said. "You're Mr. Cain, aren't you?

"Just Lucas, ma'am," Lucas said. "I'd rather be called Lucas."

Sally giggled and took a drink. "Lucas," she said. "All right, I'll call you Lucas." She put her hand up to his face and ran her finger across his lips. Lucas started to push her hand away but he tolerated it.

"Ohhh," Sally said, making the word one long exhalation. The tip of her tongue darted out to lick her lips and her nostrils flared slightly. Her eyes, which were old beyond their years, widened.

Lucas reached up to take her hand in his and move it away from his face.

"You don't like that?" Sally asked.

"No," he answered simply.

At the front of the saloon, the batwing doors swung open and three men came in. Lucas recognized them at once, and he tensed, ready for anything.

Two of the men were the ones who had been dogging him on the way into Winning Hand, Ray and Gus. The other was his one-time partner, Deke Pauley. Deke saw Lucas and came straight to his table. He smiled at Lucas, but it wasn't the same, friendly smile he had given before. This time it had a brittle edge to it. The friendship was over.

Lucas put his hands under the table. "Hello, Deke," he said. "What brings you into town?"

"I've got some business I need to take care of," Deke said.

"It's a little late in the day to take care of business, isn't it? Everything is closed. "

"*You're* the business," Deke said.

"Yeah, I sort of thought I might be."

"Mr. Tudway says you turned down his generous offer to come work for him."

"That's right."

"Mr. Tudway wants me to tell you that you aren't welcome on Winning Hand anymore."

Lucas smiled. "Hell, Deke, what's so different about that? I wasn't welcome the last time I came out there."

"You sort of sneaked up on us the last time," Deke said. "But I want you to know that from now on, I'll have my people out looking just for you."

"I hope you have somebody smarter than these two dumb apes," Lucas said, nodding toward Gus and Ray.

"Who are you callin' dumb apes, mister?" Ray asked.

"There're not only dumb, they don't hear very well, either," Lucas said.

"Listen, mister, I think you ought to know that if I would've known that Mr. Tudway didn't care whether you was dead or alive, you would've never got the drop on me," Ray said. "You'd be dead now."

"Enough of that, Ray," Pauley said. He turned back to Lucas. "Lucas, you do get my message, don't you? If I ever see you out on Winning Hand land again, I'm going to have to stop you."

"Is the kid out there?" Lucas asked.

"The kid? Oh, you mean the Mexican brat?" Pauley replied. "Yeah. Yeah, he's out there. But you don't need to worry about him. He's bein' well took care of."

"Mrs. Davenport wants the boy brought back to Davenport Court."

"Yeah, well, if she wants the kid, all she has to do is pay the price."

"She's already paid the price," Lucas said, smiling without mirth."

"What do you mean she's already paid the price?"

"She paid it to me," Lucas explained. "I'm going to get the kid back for her."

"Don't do it, Lucas. If you try, I'm going to have to kill you," Pauley said. Now it was his time to smile. "And I don't like killin' my friends. It puts me off my feed."

"I'm gonna kill 'im for you."

Pauley looked over at Ray. "You're going to do it?"

"Yeah, I'm going to do it," Ray answered. "He don't look so tough to me. How about it, Cain? What do you say? You want to try it now? Go for your gun." Ray moved his hand down to hover just over his own gun.

The conversation had started easily enough, but it had quickly progressed to a dangerous level, and now a challenge had been issued. Sally, suddenly realizing what Ray was doing, gasped and got up from the table, moving away so quickly that she knocked over the chair she had been sitting in. From another table, a woman's laughter halted in mid trill and the piano player pulled his hands away from the keyboard so that the last three notes of his melody hung raggedly, discordantly, in the air. All conversations ceased and everyone in the crowded saloon turned to see if the event they had all been speculating on was about to take place. Some of them were disappointed to see that the confrontation was between Lucas and Ray, not Lucas and Pauley.

"Now wait a minute, Ray. That is your name, isn't it? Ray?"

"That's the name," Ray said.

"Well, Ray, it wouldn't be a fair draw now, would it?" Lucas asked, replying to the man's challenge. "I mean, I'm sitting down and you're standing up. I couldn't get to my gun fast enough."

Ray's smile broadened. "Yeah, well, that's the way of it. Sometimes you just got to take it the way it comes. Now, Mr. Cain, I told you to go for your gun and I ain't goin' to wait all night for you to do it."

Lucas smiled up at Ray and his smile was even colder and more frightening than that of the man who was challenging him.

"Well, Ray, the truth is, I don't have to go for my gun. I already have it out," he said. "You see, I figured you might try somethin' like this, so I got ready for you. I'm holding a gun underneath this table right now and it's pointed straight at your gut."

Ray blinked a couple of times, then he laughed nervously. "Who the hell are you trying to kid, mister?" he asked. "You ain't got no gun in your hand. You're bluffin'."

"I might be," Lucas said.

"You expect me to believe you?"

"I hope you don't believe me," Lucas said. "I hope you try me, so we can get this over with and I can get back to my supper."

Ray stood his ground for a moment longer, trying to decide whether or not he would call Lucas's bluff. His eyes narrowed, a muscle in his cheek twitched, and sweat broke out on his forehead.

"What are you going to do now, Ray?" Gus asked.

"I don't know," Ray admitted. "What do you think, Pauley? You know him. Does he have a holdout gun under there?"

"I don't know whether he does or not," Pauley said easily.

Ray smiled. "I don't think he does. Come on, Pauley, let's me and you call his bluff."

"Uh-uh," Pauley said. *"You* started it. *You* call his bluff."

"But you said he doesn't have a gun under there."

"No. What I said was, I didn't know if he had one or not. What I *do* know is I'm not going to call his bluff."

"You mean you're just goin' to hang me out to dry?" Ray asked anxiously.

"It's not my fight," Pauley replied.

"Gus?" Ray asked.

"Leave me out of it," Gus said. "This is all your doin'."

"Damn!" Ray shouted. He put his hands out in front of him. "All right, all right, I ain't goin' to go for my gun right now," he said. He pointed at Lucas. "But you and me has got us a score to settle, mister. And I don't plan on just waitin' around till you come onto Winning Hand land before it's settled."

"Come on, Ray, Gus, let's get out of here," Pauley said.

"Deke?" Lucas called out as the three men started to leave. Deke turned toward Lucas.

"Tell Tudway I'll give him until seven o'clock in the morning to bring the kid into town. If the kid's not here by then, I'm coming out there to get him."

"You don't want to do that, Lucas," Deke said.

"I'm going to do it."

"You're just one man. What do you expect to do?"

"I expect to make Tudway's life so miserable that when I finally send that sorry son of a bitch to hell, he'll welcome the change."

"Do you think that's supposed to scare Mr. Tudway?" Ray said.

Pauley waved Ray quiet. "Shut up, Ray," he said, then turned to Lucas. "Don't be a fool, Lucas. Don't you know that if you come out there, I'm goin' to have to kill you?"

"I know you're going to try," Lucas said. "But you have to know that I'm going to be trying just as hard not to get killed."

"You'll lose, Lucas. I'll have an army waiting for you."

"If your army is no better than these two, you won't have much," Lucas said.

"You son of a bitch!" Ray started, but Pauley reached out to grab him.

"That's enough," Pauley said. "We've got to get back to the ranch. We've got to make preparations for our…" He paused and smiled without mirth at Lucas. "Visitor," he concluded, letting the word slide out slowly.

Lucas watched until all three of the men had disappeared through the swinging batwing doors, then he brought his hands up from under the table. He had been holding a pistol in his hand, and had been prepared to use it. He slipped it back into his holster.

Sally came back over to Lucas's table and picked up the chair she had knocked over a moment earlier.

"You told him to have the kid in town by seven in the morning," she said. "If they don't, are you really going out there after him?"

"That's right."

"Don't do it," Sally pleaded. "I saw Pauley in action the other night. He's very fast, you know."

"Yes, I know."

"He's very good."

"Yes, he is," Lucas said again.

"What if he's faster than you?"

"I could get killed," Lucas answered.

"Do you want to get killed?" Sally asked, frustrated because she couldn't get through to him.

"No."

"Then why are you doing it? That kid doesn't mean anything to you."

Lucas smiled broadly. "That's where you're wrong," he said. "That kid means a lot to me. I'm gettin' paid to bring him in."

"Not even money means something if you're dead. You're crazy, do you know that?"

"I've had a few people tell me that, from time to time." Lucas stood up then.

"Where are you going?"

"To get a hotel room. I can't stay up all night if I'm going out to the Winning Hand tomorrow."

"You don't need a hotel room," Sally said seductively.

Lucas smiled. "Like I said, I can't stay awake all night."

Like a raging bull, Ray suddenly came barging back into the saloon, pushing his way through the batwing doors.

"Draw, Cain, you low-life son of a bitch!" he shouted. He pointed his pistol, already drawn toward the table where Cain had been sitting. It was obvious that he expected Lucas to still be where he had left him but moments earlier. For a second he was confused by the fact that the table was empty.

Lucas heard the challenge, and spun around quickly, his hand dipping for his gun even as he turned. He saw Ray, gun in hand, looking in dumb confusion at the empty table.

"I'm over here, Ray," Lucas called easily, almost conversationally.

Ray whirled toward the stairs, whipping his gun around and firing in the same motion. His bullet crashed into the mug of beer the piano player had sitting on top of his upright, sending up a shower of glass and amber fluid. The piano player, suddenly finding himself in the middle of a gunfight, dived to the floor and scooted underneath the nearest table. At the same time Sally screamed and started running toward the stairs. Everyone else gave way, like the sea at Moses's command, so that nothing was between Ray and Lucas. All this activity was unnecessary. For even as they were in midmotion Lucas had already joined the fray.

Lucas's pistol had come out of his holster like a striking rattlesnake. He pulled the trigger as soon as the pistol was in position, and an orange flash, followed by a blossom of white smoke erupted from the muzzle.

Ray caught a slug in his chest. Convulsively, he fired one more time, but his bullet punched harmlessly into the floor. Ray's eyes glazed and he staggered sideways, then crashed through an empty table, breaking it into two pieces as he fell. He landed flat on the floor, the still-smoking gun in his hand. His mouth was open and a little sliver of blood oozed down his chin. Though his body was still jerking a bit, his eyes were open and unseeing.

Lucas, still holding his pistol, kept his eyes on the door lest

---

DEKE OR GUS, or both of them, decided to follow Ray. Apparently, they had no interest in doing so, for neither of them showed up.

"Sheriff! Sheriff!" someone shouted from out in the street. "Sheriff, there's been a shootin' over at the Golden Eagle!"

Lucas walked over to the bar and leaned against it, still keeping his eyes on the door. Without being asked, the bartender poured a drink, then slid the glass down to Lucas. Lucas picked it up and tossed it down. Heavy footfalls sounded on the boardwalk in front of the saloon, then the batwing doors swung open and Sheriff Slater stepped inside. He looked down at the body, then over at Lucas.

"I don't reckon I even need to ask who done this," he said.

"I don't reckon," Lucas said.

"He didn't have no choice, Slater," the bartender said. "This fella on the floor come in through the door, gunnin' for 'im."

Sheriff Slater rubbed his chin, then sighed. "All right," he said. "Couple of you men get this stiff down to the undertaker's establishment." He looked over at Lucas.

"Mr. Cain, I hope you ain't plannin' on hangin' around my town much longer. You're hard on the population."

"I won't be around long," Lucas said.

"How long?"

"I'll be gone in the morning."

"Yeah. I heard you give Tudway a deadline," Sheriff Baker said. "What if he don't bring the kid in by then?"

"I'll be gone in the morning," Lucas repeated.

14

Lucas was awakened the next morning by the sound of the train whistle. He got out of bed, then dressed quickly and left, closing the door softly behind him. He moved along the upstairs hallway of the Golden Eagle Saloon, listening to the snorers and heavy breathing of the overnight guests in the other rooms. As he walked down the stairway, the cacophony of snoring gradually fell behind him to be replaced by the measured *tick-tock* of the clock behind the bar. Its workings sounded exceptionally loud in the early-morning emptiness of the saloon. The clock showed that it was ten minutes to six. That meant Lucas had time to eat breakfast before the seven o'clock deadline he had given Tudway to return the boy.

As Lucas left the saloon he saw the train that had awakened him. The locomotive sat hissing and popping while its smokestack spewed forth a billowing cloud of black smoke. This was a freight train and already several wagons were in line, waiting for their turn. Some were taking cargo from the train, others were putting cargo on.

The Chuckwagon Café was across the street from the saloon, and when Lucas went inside, he saw that there were only four other customers at this early hour. Two of them were teamsters whose wagon, standing empty in front of the café, had not yet joined the queue down at the depot. The other two diners were a couple of drummers, waiting for the morning stage. Their samples cases sat on the floor beside them.

Lucas ordered a stack of pancakes, two eggs, a large piece of ham, biscuits, and red-eye gravy. It was quite a breakfast, but when Lucas was on the trail he ate so irregularly and modestly that he tended to make up for it when the opportunity presented itself. He was halfway through his breakfast when someone opened the door of the café and called out to the two teamsters.

"Lenny, Amos? All the rest of the wagons are gone. They're ready for you guys if you want to move your wagon down there now."

"All right, we'll be right there," one of them said, finishing his coffee in one big swig.

"What's goin' on, Lenny? You two boys know someone in the railroad to have a special invitation like that?" one of the drummers teased.

"Nothin' special about it," Lenny answered. "We're just pickin' up a load of dynamite, that's all. Nobody else likes to be around when that stuff is being handled."

"Yeah," Amos added, laughing. "We got us a free breakfast out of it. The other drivers got together and bought our breakfast if we'd agree to wait until they was gone."

"You say you're handling dynamite? Well, I can't say

as I blame them for wantin' to be out of there before you started," the drummer said.

"Oh, dynamite's not bad," Lenny said. "I mean, it ain't like handlin' nitro. You really got to be careful with that stuff."

"You boys come back," the proprietor of the café called out as the teamsters left. "But don't you be bringin' any dynamite with you," he added with a smile.

Lucas lingered over his breakfast for another twenty minutes are so, drinking two extra cups of coffee. He had told Tudway that he would give him until seven o'clock, and he intended to do just that.

"Would you like anything else from the kitchen, Mr. Cain? Another stack of pancakes, perhaps?"

"No, thanks. Is that clock right?" he asked, nodding toward the clock on the wall.

"Yes, sir, fifteen minutes until seven," the proprietor said, pulling out his own pocket watch and comparing the two. "That clock keeps time to the minute," he added proudly. "Why, even the folks down at the depot sometimes come down here to check on the time."

Lucas put some money down on the table to pay for his breakfast, then stood up. He harbored no false hope that Tudway would meet his deadline. Nevertheless, he intended to be out in the street in plenty of time to meet him, just as if he believed it might actually happen.

Just down the street from the Chuckwagon, in front of Tudway's Emporium, the two teamsters who had been in the café had already taken the cargo off the train and were now unloading their wagon. From the delicate way they were handling the boxes, Lucas knew it was the dynamite they had been talking about.

"Lucas!" a woman's voice shouted, and Lucas looked around to see Mrs. Davenport coming toward him, moving as quickly as her old legs would carry her. "Lucas, come quick!"

At first Lucas thought perhaps the boy had been delivered, but the tone in her voice was more of anguish than of joy. He started toward her.

"What is it?" he asked. "What's wrong?"

"It's Malcolm," Mrs. Davenport said.

Lucas followed Mrs. Davenport back to her private car. Even before he got there, though, he could see a crowd of people standing around, looking down at something on the ground. When he was close enough, he saw that they were looking at a body. It was Malcolm.

"When did this happen?" Lucas asked.

"It must have just happened," Mrs. Davenport said. "Poor Malcolm left the car no more than five minutes ago. He said he was going after water. He wasn't gone more than a couple of minutes when I heard a bump outside. I came out to see what it was, and I found him, just like this."

Malcolm, fully dressed in his striped pants and long-tailed coat, was lying face down in the dirt. A swarm of flies had already been attracted to the blood that had formed a pool beneath him, and they were buzzing about excitedly.

Lucas kneeled beside the old man's body and rolled him over. There was a knife sticking out of his chest, and the people who were standing around gasped when they saw it. Their gasps turned to exclamations of surprise and curiosity, however, when they saw that the knife was holding a note.

Lucas removed the knife, and read the note: *"Mrs. Davenport, if you want the boy, you are going to have to pay the price."*

"Oh, my," Mrs. Davenport said. She began to dab at

her eyes. "Oh, my, I caused this. Poor Malcolm. He was such a dear, sweet soul. He never hurt anyone in his life. All he wanted to do was help others. How could I have let this get this far? How could I have done this to him?"

"You didn't do this to him," Lucas said. "Tudway did it. Or he had it done, and that's the same thing."

"How could anyone do this?" she asked.

"You would be surprised at how easy this is for some people," Lucas said. He folded the note and put it in his pocket.

"Make way! Make way, here! Let me through!" Sheriff Slater shouted as he pushed his way through the crowd. When he saw Lucas, he let out a long, exasperated sigh. "What the hell is it with you, Cain?" he asked. "Everywhere you go, somebody turns up dead. Did you do this?"

"No," Lucas said.

"He's tellin' the truth, Sheriff," Lenny said. "When Amos an' me come down here to pick up our load, Cain was still eatin' his breakfast. Sometime later, me an' Amos seen that there fancy-dressed dead feller there, out of this here private car."

"Did you see who did this to him?" the sheriff asked.

"No," Amos answered. "Like Lenny said, we just seen him come out of the private car, that's all. By then we had our stuff all loaded, so we took it down to the emporium. A couple minutes later we seen Cain, come out of the restaurant and talk to Mrs. Davenport. So he couldn't 've had nothin' to do with it."

"Did anybody see anything?" the sheriff asked in an exasperated tone of voice.

No one volunteered an answer.

The sheriff looked at Lucas. "I thought you said you were goin' to be gone this morning."

"That's what I said."

"It's morning."

"All right, I'm going," Lucas said.

"Good," the sheriff said. He looked at the two teamsters. "Lenny, how about you and Amos take this fella down to the undertaker? I guess Gene can bury this one along with the one got hisself killed last night."

"That won't be necessary, Sheriff," Mrs. Davenport said. "I intend to take Malcolm's body back to Davenport Court and bury it alongside my husband." She dabbed her eyes again. "I'm sure that's where he would like to be."

"Are you leavin' right away?"

"No," Mrs. Davenport said. "I'm going to wait here until Mr. Cain returns."

"Returns? Returns from where?"

"From an errand he is doing for me," Mrs. Davenport said.

"Some errand," the sheriff said. "You're goin' to get yourself killed, that's what you're goin' to do." He looked back at Mrs. Davenport. "Well, if you ain't goin' back right away, you at least want the undertaker to put this man in a box and hold him for you, don't you?"

"Yes," Mrs. Davenport said, and at her comment the two teamsters went about the task the sheriff had assigned them.

"All right, folks," the sheriff said. "You can break it up now. Go on about your business, the show's over."

As the crowd started to leave, Mrs. Davenport called Lucas to one side so she could speak to him privately. Lucas stepped over to hear her. "Mr. Cain, I told you I would pay you ten thousand dollars to bring Roberto back," she said. "I want the boy alive and I want him unhurt. But if for some reason you can't do that, then

I'll pay the ten thousand dollars to see Jules Tudway dead."

"I don't kill for hire, Mrs. Davenport," Lucas reminded her.

"And I'm not hiring you to kill him, Mr. Cain. I'm just putting a bounty on him, that's all. If in the course of your job, Jules Tudway is killed, I will pay that bounty."

"That's a pretty narrow point," Lucas said.

"Yes, I agree," Mrs. Davenport replied. She smiled coldly. "But you might say that I am a narrow-minded woman. I want that man dead."

"I'm sure you do. But don't forget, there is a man standing between Tudway and me who might have other ideas."

"You're talking about Pauley?"

"Yes," Lucas said.

"How loyal do you think he would really be if it came right down to it?" Mrs. Davenport asked.

"Loyalty has nothing to do with it," Lucas said. "For Pauley, Tudway is the goose that is laying the golden eggs. He isn't going to want to see that goose killed."

"You and Pauley were friends once, weren't you?"

"I like to think that we're still friends. We're just on different sides of this situation."

"You're better than Pauley, aren't you?" Mrs. Davenport asked.

"I don't know," Lucas admitted. "But I'm afraid we're going to find out."

It took Lucas less than five minutes to saddle his horse and about ten more minutes to pick up a few supplies at the emporium. The storekeeper raised his eyes at some of the items, then raised them again when Lucas told him to send the bill to Mrs. Davenport. The emporium may have belonged to Tudway, but for the storekeeper the bottom line was profit. Therefore, he made no effort to deny Lucas his purchases, no matter what they may have been. As a result, Lucas had everything he needed to wage war against Winning Hand Ranch, and when he left town fifteen minutes later, he was ready for business

---

"I WANT a lookout posted in the loft of the barn at all times," Deke Pauley said. "I want another one on top of the big house. And get somebody to build a little shelf up in the cottonwood tree, by the boy's window." Pauley was standing out on the plaza at Winning Hand, looking up at Gus, who was seated on his horse.

"Hell, what do we need all that for? We already got somebody down at the pass," Gus said. He reached down and patted his horse's neck. "There ain't nobody that can get through there without us knowing about it."

"Nevertheless, I want you to do what I said. And the barn, too. I want one man in the loft and another on the roof. Now, what about the rifle pits? How are they comin'?"

Gus laughed. "What's all the fuss, Pauley? You act like we was about to get attacked by an army or somethin'. Lookouts, rifle pits. You sure you don't have a couple of cannons hid out somewhere?"

"Believe me, if I had them, I would use them," Pauley replied. "And as far as you're concerned, Cain *is* an army. A one-man army."

"He ain't no different from anyone else. I'll bet you're faster than he is. And anyway, when it comes right down to it, he puts his pants on one leg at a time just like ever'one else."

"How do you know that?" Pauley replied. "You ever seen him put his pants on?"

"Well, no, but..."

"I have," Pauley said. "He ain't like ever'body else."

"Are you afraid of him, Pauley?"

"You damn right, I'm afraid of him. You would be too if you had any sense. Now, do like I told you."

"But you're faster," Gus insisted. "I mean, ever'body says that."

"Do they?"

"Well, aren't you?"

"We'll never know that until the issue is put to the test, will we? Now, get busy."

"All right, all right," Gus said. "I'll get the lookouts all posted and I'll see to it that the rifle pits are dug, and if you want me to, I'll see if I can find a cannon or two for you."

"Just do it."

Pauley watched Gus ride off, then a moment later, he heard someone walking up behind him.

"You keep on talking like that, you're going to scare everyone to death," Tudway said, lighting a cheroot. He shook the match out before he tossed it away.

"I want everyone to be afraid of him," Pauley said. "I want them to think he's part grizzly bear, part mountain lion, and part Apache all rolled into one."

"I've heard of him, of course," Tudway said. "But I wonder. Is he really that good, or is the only thing we know about him a bunch of tall tales that get taller with each tellin'?"

Pauley fixed Tudway with a long hard stare.

"You forget, me 'n him rode together for a while. He's that good," he finally said.

"Too bad," Tudway said. "Too bad we couldn't talk him into working for us. Especially if he's as good as you say he is. If he's the best."

Pauley pulled the makings out of his pocket and began rolling a cigarette.

"I didn't say he was the best," Pauley said as he sprinkled the tobacco into the paper. "He's damn good," he added as he licked the paper and rolled it closed, twisting each end. "But the question of who is the best is still unanswered."

"Who do *you* think is the best?" Tudway asked.

"Whoever is left alive when all this is over," Pauley answered.

15

The night was thick with tension as Lucas Cain stealthily made his way through the terrain surrounding the dam. Jules Tudway had built the dam to divert water away from the neighboring farms and towns, leaving the land dry and barren.

Lucas moved with the expertise of a predator as he silently approached the dam. He reached a vantage point overlooking the dam but was still obscured by the willows that had grown up close to the water.

Lucas unpacked a small satchel, revealing sticks of dynamite and a length of fuse. He surveyed the dam looking for the precise spots where he could do the most damage. He knew that destroying the dam was the only way to restore the natural flow of water to the towns, farms, and ranches downstream.

With careful precision, he placed the dynamite at key points along the dam's base, ensuring that the explosive force would be enough to crack the structure. The night air was charged with anticipation as Lucas worked quickly but methodically.

As he attached the final stick of dynamite, Lucas paused, listening for any signs of approaching danger. The distant howls of coyotes and the rustle of leaves in the wind were the only sounds he could hear. Satisfied that he had not been detected, he lit the fuse, the flame flickering in the darkness.

With the fuse burning, Lucas moved back to a safe position, his eyes fixed on the dam. He took a deep breath and waited while the burning fuse crept closer. Then, with a deafening roar, the dynamite exploded, sending shockwaves through the night.

Water surged from the breach, tearing down the weakened dam. Lucas watched as the torrent of water cascaded downstream. The rushing water would be the first strike to the end of Tudway's tyranny.

Lucas knew that his actions would draw the ire of Jules Tudway and his henchmen, but in that moment, Lucas Cain stood unafraid. As the water continued to flow, the landowners below would awaken to the life-giving gift that had been stolen from them. With a silent nod to the rush of water, Lucas Cain slipped away into the quiet of the night, ready to face whatever consequences awaited him. That morning, like every morning, the cook at Winning Hand Ranch made biscuits for breakfast, kneaded dough for bread for the rest of the day, peeled potatoes, carved meat, cleaned the stove, and attended to the dozen or more other duties for which he was responsible. By the time the other hands were sitting down for their breakfast, the cook was already three hours into his day.

On this morning, the cook put the bacon, eggs, potatoes, biscuits, and coffee on the table so the men could help themselves. With that taken care of, he took a couple of sheets of old newspaper with him and started out to the toilet. The newspaper would give him something to read while he was doing his business, and, of course, it would come in handy afterward.

The toilet was on the other side of the stream, away from the water so as not to contaminate it. Unlike most of the other ranches in the area, Winning Hand enjoyed an ample supply of water. That was because of the dozen or more streams and tributaries that branched off from the Diablo River. These streams and tributaries weren't natural offshoots from the river; they had been created when Tudway dammed up the river. Normally, such a damn would have backed the water up until a large lake was formed, but that was prevented by a system of sluices and gates that rerouted the water.

This elaborate water system was good for Winning Hand, for it brought water to even the most remote part of the ranch. However, it was bad for the other ranchers and farmers in the valley because the same dam that created the Winning Hand irrigation system caused the Diablo to stop flowing. No one downstream of Winning Hand, not one rancher, received so much as one drop of water from the Diablo. In fact, Tudway had built the cookhouse and granary right in the dry riverbed through which the Diablo once flowed. A small tributary still managed to get through, and by building the granary there, Tudway could harness its energy to turn the waterwheel that ground his grain. The little stream also provided the water the cook needed to run his kitchen, and fed the water tank in the middle of the plaza. It was that same stream the cook crossed when he left the kitchen to go to the toilet.

The cook had been sitting in the toilet for a few minutes when he heard the sound. It sounded a little like thunder, deep and resonant, way up in the hills. And yet it wasn't quite like thunder; it had a flatter, more immediate sound. Besides, there wasn't a cloud in the sky.

There was another thump soon after the first, and this time it made the hairs stand up on the back of the cook's neck. That was because he had heard a sound like this before during the war. This sounded exactly like artillery. But that was crazy. Why would anyone be shooting out here?

The cook made a quick, final use of the paper, then stepped out of the toilet and looked up toward the hills. He saw an ominous little puff of smoke hanging just on the other side of one of the notches in the hills and it puzzled him. Then he heard a rushing noise that puzzled him even more. He strained and stared.

"Oh, my god!" he shouted. He started toward the little bridge, yelling at the men in the cookhouse. "Get out! Get out of there! Get out!"

The rushing noise the cook had heard was now a loud roar as five hundred yards away, a mighty torrent of water rolled, tumbled, and cascaded down the mountainside, refilling the dry channel.

The wall of water rounded the final bend in the old riverbed, then rushed pell-mell toward the ranch buildings. It smashed into the granary, knocked in the walls, then continued on, sweeping away the wheat, oats, and corn that had been stored there.

By now, the roar of water was so loud that even the cowboys at breakfast could hear it, and a few managed to run out the door before the cookhouse, like the granary, was knocked off its foundation and swept downstream. There were several cowboys still trapped inside the cookhouse and suddenly they found themselves fighting against the stove, table, and chairs that were being tossed around. Finally, they too managed to escape, dodging the swirling pieces of debris and swimming madly for dry land. Eventually, all of them made it to safety, though several of them lay on the ground, wet as drowned rats and gasping for breath.

Deke Pauley had not been caught in the flood. He lived in the foreman's house, separate from the kitchen and from the big house. He had spent the entire day the day before looking for Lucas Cain, puzzled by the fact that Lucas had not made an appearance. He knew that the incident with Mrs. Davenport's man hadn't scared Lucas off, and he had told Tudway that it wouldn't. However, Tudway had insisted that it be done, and since Pauley was taking his money and his orders from Tudway, he did it. Though most wouldn't recognize it, Pauley did have a code of honor and that code of honor dictated that if he took money for a job, he would do the job, even if he didn't see the sense of it. He had killed the valet, even though he hadn't seen the sense of it.

Since Lucas had not shown up on Winning Hand land on the day before, Pauley slept very little during the night. He had expected Lucas at any moment and he was alert to every sound and every movement all night long. As a result, he was still pretty groggy when he awakened, much too groggy to take breakfast with the men. He had gone over to the cookhouse a few minutes earlier to get a biscuit and a cup of coffee, which he took back with him. Then, when he heard the noise of the explosions, he groaned because he knew immediately what was happening. Now he stood on the front porch of his house and watched as the wreckage of the granary and cookhouse rolled and tumbled down the stream.

"What is it? What's going on?" Tudway yelled as he rushed outside, pulling galuses up over his shoulders. When he saw a river where moments before a dry bed had been, he cursed out loud. "Son of a bitch! Where did that come from?"

"It came from Lucas Cain," Pauley said.

"Cain? How?" Tudway sputtered.

"He blew the dams," Pauley said.

"Pauley, what is this? You said we could scare him off. He didn't even show up yesterday, did he? And yesterday was the deadline."

"*You* said we could scare him off, Mr. Tudway," Pauley said. "*I* didn't."

"Who does he think he is? What does he think he's doing, blowing my dams like that?"

"He thinks he's declared war on us, Mr. Tudway," Pauley said.

"Oh, he does, does he? Well, I'll give that son of a bitch war. Get the men mounted," Tudway ordered. "Get them mounted now and go out there after him. I want his hide nailed to my barn door."

"Don't you think it would be better if I went up by myself?" Pauley asked. "Or with just one or two of the men that I pick?"

"No, I don't think it would be better!" Tudway responded angrily. "You looked for him all day yesterday, didn't you? And you didn't find him, did you? I want Cain to know who he's tangling with. And that means that I want every man who can ride in the saddle out looking for him."

"You aren't talking about the cowboys too, are you? Don't you mean just my men?"

"No, I want the cowboys, I want everybody, do you understand? I want that son of a bitch stopped and I want him stopped now."

"Yes, sir," Pauley said, expressing by the tone of his voice that he believed Tudway was making a mistake.

"Men," Tudway shouted to the cowboys who were still milling about and picking through the wreckage that had been deposited along the banks of the river. "I want Lucas Cain! Do you hear me? I want Lucas Cain! You bring him back to me, dead or alive, and it's worth five hundred dollars to every man here."

"Do you mean five hundred dollars a man?" one of the cowboys wanted to know.

"That's what I mean. Five hundred dollars for each and every man," Tudway repeated. "Plus a bounty of five thousand dollars to the man who actually gets him."

"Five thousand?" one of the men asked, astounded by the figure.

"Five thousand to the one who gets him," Tudway repeated.

"Yahoo! Let's go! Let's go get the bastard!" one of the cowboys shouted. All the men hurried to the barn to saddle up.

It took nearly ten minutes for all of them to get saddled and ready to ride. Finally, with many of them still dripping wet from their dunking in the river, they were ready to go. Pauley sat in front of them, a reluctant general to the small army.

"All right, men," Pauley said. "You know who we're after. Let's go get him."

"I've got the rope!" somebody shouted. "We'll hang the son of a bitch."

Several of the others let out a yell and nearly two dozen horsemen started out at a gallop. Pauley went with them, but when he caught Gus's eye, he shook his head in quiet frustration.

THE RIDERS GALLOPED until their blood cooled, their enthusiasm waned, and their horses grew tired. Then one of the cowboys realized that they were just running with no sense of direction or purpose. He pulled up, and because he was at the front of the pack, the others came to a halt with him.

"What is it, what's goin' on?" someone asked.

"Why'd we stop?"

The rider who had caused the others to stop looked over at Pauley. "You're the boss of this outfit, Pauley. What do you think we ought to do now?" he asked. "I mean, we can't just go on a-runnin' around out here like chickens with our heads cut off."

"You finally figured that out, did you?" Pauley asked.

"Yeah," the cowboy answered sheepishly. He reached down and patted the neck of his horse. "I guess we did run off there half-cocked."

"Well, what now?" one of the others asked. "I mean, I ain't flatterin' myself that I'm the one who'll get the five thousand dollars. But I ain't ready to just give up on that five hundred we'll all get if somebody else gets him."

"Does that mean you're ready to listen to me?" Pauley asked.

"Yeah, are you kiddin'? For five hundred dollars, we'll listen."

"All right then. We're goin' to divide up," Pauley said. About three or four of you to a group. That way we can spread out and cover more territory."

"What do we do if we find him?" someone asked.

"If you find him and you can kill him, you'll divide the five thousand among you," Pauley said simply.

"Yeah, yeah, that's for me," someone said. "I'm all for killin' the son of a bitch. That bastard nearly drowned me. And besides, he's worth just as much to us dead as he is alive."

Within a moment there were as many as five smaller groups, fanning out in all different directions. Now, with a sense of direction and purpose, their enthusiasm returned.

"Come on, Gus," Pauley said. "You, Austin, and Dudley come with me."

"Where we goin'?"

"We're goin' back to the big house," Pauley said. "If Cain is after the kid, that's where he's goin' to be headin'."

"What about these here other fellers?" Gus asked, pointing to the men who were riding off on their own missions. "You just goin' to let them go off on their own?"

"Hell, yes, let the fools go," Pauley said. "We're better off rid of 'em."

LUCAS CAIN SAW a little group of men coming after him. He was sitting calmly on top of a large round rock, watching, as four riders approached a narrow draw. The draw was so confined that they would not be able to get through without squeezing into a single file. It was a place that no one with any tactical sense would go. These were not men with a sense of tactics, however. These were cowboys, fired up by the promise of a five-hundred-dollar reward for bringing in Lucas Cain, dead or alive. There wasn't a one of them who really intended that Lucas should be brought in alive. And there wasn't a one of them who would balk at putting a noose around Lucas's neck.

Because of that, they were men who could be easily lured into a trap.

Cain stood up so that he could clearly be seen against the skyline.

"Look! There he is!"

"He's up there!"

"Let's get him! Let's get the son of a bitch!"

The riders galloped through the draw, bent on capturing or killing Lucas Cain.

A couple of the men in front thought that Lucas made an easy target, so they pulled their pistols and began shooting up toward him as they rode. Lucas could see the flash of the gunshots, then the little puffs of dust as the bullets hit. The spent bullets whined as they ricocheted on by him, though none of the missiles came close enough to cause him to duck.

Lucas was smoking a cigar and now he leaned over, almost casually, to light two fuses. A little starburst of sparks started at each fuse, then ran sputtering and snapping along the length of fuse for several feet alongside the draw. The first explosion went off about fifty yards in front of the lead rider, a heavy, stomach-shaking thump that filled the draw with smoke and dust, then brought a ton of rocks crashing down to close the draw so that the riders couldn't get through.

The second explosion was somewhat less powerful, located behind the riders. It too brought rocks crashing down into the draw behind them, closing the passage up. Lucas chuckled. It was going to be a long, slow process before the cowboys would be able to dig their way out of this.

Lucas scrambled down off the rock, then wriggled through a fissure that was just large enough to allow a man to pass through if he weren't riding. He had left Charley Three on the other side, and now he mounted and rode on, leaving the trapped cowboys behind him.

Lucas rode no more than a quarter of a mile before he saw the next group of riders. Attracted by the sounds of the explosions, they were hurrying over to see what it was.

"There he is!" someone shouted, pointing at Lucas.

"Get him!" another yelled.

All four riders started after Lucas at a full gallop.

Lucas took his horse into a mesquite thicket. The limbs slapped painfully against his face and arms but they closed behind him too, so that he was hidden from view. Lucas slowed his horse just enough to hop off, then he slapped him on the haunch, sending him on. Lucas squatted down behind a mesquite bush and waited.

In less than ten minutes, his pursuers came by. Lucas reached up and grabbed the fourth rider and jerked him off his horse. The man gave a short, startled cry as he was going down, but the cry was cut off when he broke his neck in the fall.

The rider just in front heard the cry and he looked around in time to see what was happening.

"Hey! He's back here!" he called. This rider had been riding with his pistol in his hand, so he was able to get off a shot at almost the same moment he yelled.

The man was either a much better shot than Lucas had anticipated or he was lucky, for the bullet grazed the fleshy part of Lucas's arm, not close enough to make a hole, but close enough to cut a deep, painful crease. The impact of the bullet, plus the effort of unseating the rider, caused Lucas to go down and he fell on his right side, thus preventing him from getting to his gun. The shooter had no such constraints, however, and he was able to get off a second shot. This time his bullet hit a mesquite limb, right in front of Lucas's face, and would have hit Lucas had the limb not been there. Lucas knew then that the first shot had not been a lucky accident. This man could shoot.

Lucas rolled hard, not only to get out of the line of fire, but to be able to reach his gun. As he pulled it up in front of him, he saw that it was covered with dirt. He had a momentary concern that the barrel might be filled with dirt, and if so, it could explode on him when he pulled the trigger. Under the circumstances, he didn't have time to worry about that. He squeezed the trigger, felt the gun pull back in his hand, then saw the shooter grab his chest and pitch backward off the horse.

The other two riders, though they had initially answered the summons of their partner, suddenly realized that in the space of a few seconds, Lucas Cain had cut the odds down to two to one. These odds weren't to their liking, so they turned and galloped away.

Lucas borrowed one of the two riderless horses to recover his own. When he tracked Charley Three down, he saw that one of the other Winning Hand groups had already found him. They had dismounted and were giving their own animals a rest. One of the riders was taking a drink from a canteen, another was leaning up against a rock holding their horses, the third was examining Lucas's horse, while the fourth was standing a short distance away relieving himself. Lucas dismounted before they saw him and sneaked up closer to them on foot.

"It's got to be his horse," one of the men said. "It sure don't belong to Winning Hand."

"How do you know?"

"It don't have a Winning Hand brand."

"Hell, what's that mean?" one of the other men asked, laughing. "Half the animals on this ranch don't have the Winning Hand brand."

"You sayin' Mr. Tudway rustles?"

"Let's just say he throws a wide loop." The others laughed. "Hell, we all do," he went on. "Else we wouldn't be workin' here. Why do you think he pays us double what any other rancher pays?"

"Newberry, what the hell you doin' over there, anyway?"

"What's it look like I'm doing?" Newberry answered. "I'm waterin' the lilies."

"You been pissin' for five minutes. At this rate, you could hire yourself out to them ranchers that can't get any water."

The others laughed.

"Why, did you see ole Newberry this mornin'?" one of the other men asked. "When he went in the river, he got as much water *in* him as *on* him."

"That's the pure truth of it," Newberry said, returning to the others as he buttoned his pants. "What do you say we backtrack this horse and try and find Cain?"

"What do you think happened to him?"

"You heard all the shootin' a while ago," Newberry said. "I figure he's either dead or wounded. Probably wounded."

"Why do you say that?"

"'Cause if he was dead, we'd know it by now. Whoever kilt him would be whoopin' and hollerin' to beat bloody hell, claimin' the extra five thousand dollars. And if he wasn't wounded, we wouldn't have his horse."

"What are we goin' to do if we find him?"

"Do? Why, we're goin' to hang the son of a bitch, that's what we're going to do." Newberry smiled. "That way *we'll* lay claim to the five thousand."

"What if he's already wounded?"

"Especially if he's already wounded," Newberry said. "If we bring him in wounded, someone else is goin' to claim it was their shot done it, and they'll be wantin' the money."

"Yeah, I guess you're right."

Lucas stepped out into the little clearing. His gun was already drawn.

"Where's Pauley?" Lucas asked.

"Damn," Newberry shouted, and he started for his pistol.

Lucas squeezed off a shot and a little mist of blood sprayed out from Newberry's arm. Newberry let out a yelp of pain and interrupted his draw to slap his hand against the source of his wound.

"You son of a bitch!" he shouted in pain and anger.

"Where's Pauley?" Lucas asked.

"I don't know," Newberry said.

Lucas cocked his pistol. "I might as well even you up," he said, pointing at Newberry's other arm.

"No, no!" Newberry shouted, holding both his hands out in front of him, showing the bloody palm of one of them. "I'd tell you if I knew, but I don't know where he went."

"Newberry's tellin' the truth, Cain," one of the other men said. "We broke up into different groups. We ain't seen Pauley since."

Lucas waited for a moment, then he eased the hammer back down on his pistol and lowered it.

"All right," he said with a sigh. "Take your guns out of the holsters and empty the loads onto the ground."

The men did as they were directed.

"You," Lucas said, pointing to the man nearest Charley Three. "Bring my horse over."

The man obliged and Lucas mounted, then looked at the other four horses.

"Let go of their reins," he ordered.

Again, Lucas's instructions were followed.

Lucas fired a couple of shots into the dirt near the horses. The animals reared up in fright and galloped off, their hooves clattering loudly on the rocky ground.

"Hey! What'd you do that for?" Newberry asked. "It's a long walk back."

"It's going to be longer," Lucas said.

"What do you mean?"

"Take off your boots."

"What? Are you crazy? I ain't givin' you my boots," one of the men said.

"You can walk without boots, or crawl without feet," Lucas said dryly. "I don't give a damn which it is." He cocked his pistol again and aimed it at the feet of one of the men.

"No, wait! Wait, we'll do it!"

All four men sat down and then began pulling off their boots. Lucas tossed a gunnysack to them.

"Put them in there and bring them to me," he said.

A moment later, one of the men handed Lucas the sack of boots.

"Thanks," Lucas said. He hooked the sack over his saddle pommel and rode away, leaving the four cursing men behind him.

Lucas rode for half a mile before he emptied the gunnysack of the cowboys' boots. Then he found an irrigation canal and noticed that as a result of his blowing the dams earlier in the day, the canal, which Tudway had built to change the natural flow of water, was nearly dried up. There was, however, enough water in it for his purposes. He dipped his kerchief into the stream and wet it so he could clean the wound in his arm.

A few minutes later, with the wound cleaned and bandaged, as well as could be managed with one hand, he remounted and rode off. He had hoped to encounter Pauley out here. That would have made it easier for him when he went after the boy. But Pauley wasn't out here, and Lucas was pretty sure he knew where he was.

16

Pauley hadn't spent a lot of time with Lucas without learning a little about the man. He knew that Lucas Cain was a person who did what he set out to do. That meant that no matter where he was now, he was going to turn up at the ranch. The boy was here and Lucas Cain was, above all else, after the boy.

Though Tudway had ordered everyone who could ride to go after Lucas, there were several cowboys who for one reason or another had not gone. Some were just coming in from nighthawk duty, others were performing some task at another part of the ranch at the time and weren't even aware of what was going on until after the impromptu posse left. Learning that Tudway had offered a five-hundred-dollar bonus to be paid to everyone as soon as Lucas was caught, even to those who stayed back, they were eager to see him brought in. Therefore, when they saw Pauley and his group come galloping back, they hurried over to find out firsthand how the search was going. Tudway was even more anxious than the cowboys and he swept them aside as he hurried to question Pauley.

"Did you get him?" Tudway asked. "Did you kill the son of a bitch?"

"Not yet," Pauley said.

"Then what the hell are you doing back here? Why aren't you out looking for him?"

"We've got men combing the entire range," Pauley answered. "Maybe someone will get lucky. But the real place to look for him is right here."

"Right here? What do you mean?"

"I mean he's goin' to come here to get the kid," Pauley said.

"Surely he won't try it now that we're on to him, will he?" Tudway said. "I mean he'd be a fool to try it right under our noses. The only way we're going to find him is to go out after him. Now, get back out there and find him."

"Mr. Tudway, you hired me to take care of this kind of business for you, didn't you?" Pauley asked. "I figure you must have some confidence that I can do it or you wouldn't have hired me in the first place. Am I right?"

"I suppose so," Tudway said.

"Then let me do my job. Otherwise, you can just pay me off and I'll be on my way."

"All right, we'll try it your way," Tudway said.

"That's more like it," Pauley said. "Now, you men, get rifles," he ordered the others. "Get into your positions. Cain's goin' to be comin' around sooner or later."

"What about the others?" one of the cowboys asked. "The ones that's still ridin' around out there."

"What about 'em?" Pauley asked.

"Shouldn't we send someone out to bring 'em back in?"

"What the hell for?" Pauley asked. "They'll just get in the way."

"But what if they find Cain?" one of the other men asked. "Will we still get our bonus? I mean, if we're not lookin' for him?"

"Mr. Tudway said the five hundred is for everyone," Pauley said.

"Yeah, but there's five thousand dollars for the one that gets him," one of the cowboys complained. "I don't see anyone who stays here collectin' that money."

"Then go out there with the others if you want to," Pauley said easily. "After all, Cain is wandering around somewhere between us and them. Who knows? You might get lucky and find him by yourself. If you do, you won't even have to split the five thousand."

"Yeah? Maybe I'll just...hey, wait a minute," the cowboy said, suddenly realizing what Pauley was saying. "There's no way I'm going to go up against Cain by myself. What good is five thousand dollars if I'm dead?"

"You're staying here?"

"Yeah, I'm staying here."

"Then do what I tell you, without any more sass," Pauley ordered.

"Sure, Pauley, whatever you say," the cowboy said.

IT WAS mid-afternoon and though the sun was midway down in the western half of the sky, it had lost neither heat nor brilliance. The men suffered from the heat and slapped at flies and gnats and squinted into the unrelenting glare of bright sunlight as they waited. The longer they waited, the more nervous they became.

Lucas knew that a long afternoon of waiting would

just increase the tension. That was one of the reasons he hadn't made any further moves once he got into position. Right now he was on a hill about two hundred yards away from the big house, and he had been there since before lunch. He knew when it was lunchtime, because the cook, who no longer had a cookhouse, had prepared his meal around the back of a chuck wagon. It was a hearty, appetizing meal and Lucas could smell the meat and potatoes from his position. His stomach growled in protest. All he had to satisfy his own hunger was a piece of jerky and a couple of swallows of water. He placated himself by remembering meals he had eaten in the past and by thinking of meals he would eat in the future. He had gone on jerky and water before, he could do it again.

After his meager meal, Lucas lay flat on his stomach, then looked through his binoculars at the activity below. He had known that he would find Pauley and a few of his gunmen here, but he was a little surprised by how many others were still around. He had thought that everyone would be out roaming all over the range country looking for him.

Though he was surprised at the number of defenders there were here at the ranch, he wasn't surprised by the preparations they had made for him. Pauley knew his business and Lucas knew the defenses would be well laid out. From this position, however, Lucas was able to make a careful survey of the defensive positions Pauley had constructed. That knowledge could come in handy when he made his move.

There were four rifle pits around the plaza, each pit containing two men, with each of the pits having an overlapping field of fire. The overlapping field of fire meant that there was no way to cross the plaza or approached the big house without coming under fire from one of the defenders.

In addition to the rifle pits, Lucas saw that Pauley had placed six more men in strategic locations. There was one man at the window on the second floor of the big house and another up on the roof just behind the castellated wall. There was a man on the roof of the foreman's house, one on the top of the barn, and another one in the hayloft. Finally, there was a firing platform built high in the cottonwood tree that stood just by the northeast corner of the house. In addition to the rifle pits and the sharpshooters' positions, Lucas saw that there were at least two more men downstairs inside the front room of the big house.

Pauley and three of his riders didn't have any specific defensive position but were located to be able to move instantly to any place where they might be needed. Reluctantly, Lucas had to congratulate Deke on constructing his defense. A good-sized army wouldn't be able to get through.

But of course, Lucas wasn't an army. He was only one man. And one man, Lucas reasoned, might be able to slip through the cracks.

Lucas had seen Tudway at lunchtime. He came out to the chuck wagon and spoke with several of the men, then went around and examined all of the defensive positions. Shortly after lunch, Tudway had disappeared back into the big house and Lucas hadn't seen him since.

Lucas took another look at all the windows of the big house. He saw the rifleman in the window on the top floor, then he swept his binoculars across the front, looking in through each window, until he came to the window nearest the big cottonwood tree. That room was particularly interesting to him, because though the curtains were open in every other room of the house, they were drawn shut in this room. He looked at the drawn curtain several times during the afternoon, and finally he was rewarded when he saw them part slightly. A young boy's face appeared at the opening. The young boy looked around curiously for a moment, then a hand appeared and pulled the boy back away from the window. The curtains were shut again.

Lucas lowered the binoculars and smiled.

"Well, so there you are, young man," he said, muttering to himself. "I've been wondering where you were keeping yourself. Or rather, where they were keeping you. You just stay put, boy. Just stay put until I come get you. I don't know if anyone told you but you're worth ten thousand dollars to me. Ten thousand bucks, just waitin' for me to walk in there and pick it up."

As the sun dipped lower in the west Lucas decided to try to improve his position. There was another protected spot off to his left, a little ridge line that protruded like a finger, pointing right at the big house. The end of the "finger" was a hundred yards closer than he was now, and from there, Lucas would be able to see more clearly what was going on. But if he was going to do it, he was going to have to do it now before it got too dark to see. To reach it, however, he would have to cross an open area about fifty yards wide.

Lucas moved back down off the rock and walked over to his horse, Charley Three. Since Lucas had gotten into position, his horse had enjoyed a fairly relaxed afternoon cropping grass. Lucas figured he should be well rested now. That was good because he was going to call on him to run the gauntlet.

"You ready, boy?" Lucas asked, patting the horse on

its neck. "I hope so because when we go, you're going to have to give me all you've got."

Gripping his pistol in his fist, Lucas put his foot in the stirrup and lifted himself up. But he didn't get into the saddle. Instead, he remained bent over, hidden behind his horse. Once he had his balance and a good hold, he urged the animal across the open area. He broke out into the clearing at a full gallop.

"There goes his horse!" someone shouted.

"Where's he at?"

"Maybe his mount got away from him."

"The hell it did! There he is, hangin' on to the side!" someone else yelled. "Shoot him! Shoot the son of a bitch!"

Knowing that he had been spotted, Lucas raised up and fired across the top of his horse.

Those who were closest began shooting, even after Lucas had made it all the way across and was completely out of their line of fire, they kept up their shooting until finally, Pauley started shouting at them to stop.

"Hold your fire, hold your fire! You're just wastin' ammunition," he shouted.

The firing fell silent.

"Where'd he go?"

"Was he hit?"

"Does anyone see him?"

"Ever'one just keep your mouth shut and your eyes open," Pauley ordered.

Lucas was in a good, secure position now. He was close enough to observe everything. Close enough even to overhear the men when they shouted at each other. Realistically, he knew this was as close as he was going to be able to get until it got dark. But with the sun already a bloodred disk low on the western horizon, he knew that darkness wasn't too far away.

Before the light finally faded, Lucas made a careful examination of the big house. Once he saw Tudway peering anxiously through the downstairs window, and once he got a glimpse of the boy. Roberto was still in the same room he had been in all day long. It was good to know where he was, though the boy might as well be in China now, for all the good it did Lucas to know. He had no idea how he was going to get to him.

Lucas figured that his best bet would be just to wait until around midnight or one. From experience he knew that shortly after midnight was the time when those on guard would be least alert. Perhaps he would get lucky and catch some of them napping.

IT WAS JUST AFTER MIDNIGHT, and the moon hung low in the ink-black sky, casting long shadows across the vast expanse of Winning Hand Ranch.

The night was heavy with tension as Lucas Cain continued to watch the house, determined to rescue young Roberto from Tudway's clutches.

Lucas moved silently, blending with the shadows, as he approached the ranch house. He could hear the distant howling of coyotes, a haunting melody to the dangerous mission ahead. The only light came from the scattered lanterns around the ranch, creating pools of dim illumination. Lucas knew he had to move quickly.

As he neared the ranch house, Lucas spotted the silhouette of a guard patrolling the perimeter. Lucas waited behind a bush until the guard passed him, then stepping out from behind the bush, Lucas brought the butt of his pistol down over the sentinel's head, knocking him unconscious.

INSIDE THE RANCH HOUSE, Jules Tudway was totally unaware as to how close Lucas was. With the reward he had posted to be paid to everyone upon Cain's death, he was certain that Lucas Cain would soon be a person of no consequence. He reveled in his malicious triumph.

The innocent five-year-old Roberto was locked in a small room, his frightened eyes wide in the darkness. Tudway's laughter echoed through the halls, sending shivers down Roberto's spine.

Outside, the night erupted in chaos. Lucas had managed to slip past some of Tudway's guards, but the rancher, alerted to the intrusion, had summoned every man at his disposal. Tudway's ranch hands, armed and agitated, formed a makeshift militia in the darkness.

It was about an hour after dark when Lucas got an unexpected break. The cowboys who had spent the day searching the range for him were just now coming back to the ranch. They were tired, hungry, and frustrated over not yet having won the five-hundred-dollar bonus they were promised. They rode boldly and irately right up to the ranch. Unfortunately for them, they made no effort to identify themselves. The men who were manning the advanced rifle pits were already so nervous that they were jumping at every shadow. They had completely forgotten about those who were out on the range and were totally surprised to see a large body of men ride up on them.

It was too dark to see and the men were too edgy by

the circumstances to exercise caution. One of them put into words what all of them thought.

"Damn! Look at that!" one of the men in the rifle pits shouted. "Cain's brought a whole army with him!"

A rifle shot rang out from one of the pits, and it was returned by the approaching horsemen, who thought that *they* were being fired at by Lucas Cain. Their return shot was answered by another and another still, until soon, the entire valley rang with the crash and clatter of rifle and pistol fire. Gun flashes lit up the night, bullets whistled, whined, and punched into horseflesh, or buried themselves deep in the chest of one or more of the hapless cowboys.

Lucas realized at once what was happening. There was no need now to wait until after midnight. He could take advantage of the opportunity that had just presented itself. As the guns banged and crashed around him, he sneaked out of his hiding position.

As Lucas looked back toward the battle, he saw the flashes of light from each gunshot, and began to make plans as to just how he would utilize this diversion to steal into the house and get the boy.

Closing in on the room where Roberto was held captive, a volley of gunfire erupted from the ranch hands. The ranch hands, caught in the crossfire of their own making, descended into chaos. Shouts of confusion mingled with the sharp cracks of gunfire. In the dark, faces were indistinguishable, and the line between friend and foe blurred.

Outside, the private war among Tudway's ranch hands raged on. Shots were fired, and desperate pleas for ceasefire went unheard. In the confusion, some of Tudway's men fell victim to friendly fire, their figures slumping to the ground as the night swallowed their cries.

In the aftermath, the ranch hands, disoriented and realizing the grave error, surveyed the scene. The once formidable force had crumbled in the face of its own misdirected fury. Tudway's twisted empire had started to unravel.

During the fighting, the barn had caught fire and the men who had been shooting from the loft and the roof had to abandon it. Now the burning barn cast an eerie, wavering orange glow over the entire scene, illuminating enough to provide shadows as targets, but not bright enough to allow anyone to be identified and thus end the confusion.

By the ambient light of the burning barn, Lucas was able to pick his way through the downstairs part of the house. When he reached the parlor, he saw Tudway. The rancher was standing just under the portrait of himself, a little behind the fireplace so that the stone façade provided him with some additional protection from the flying bullets. Lucas couldn't help but draw an unflattering comparison between the man who was cowering behind the fireplace and the heroic figure who was portrayed in the painting above the fireplace.

There were two other men in the parlor with Tudway. They were standing at the window, looking out at the fighting that was going on outside.

"What's going on out there, Austin? Dudley? Can either of you see anything?" Tudway asked.

"Not a blasted thing," Austin answered. "Except the burning barn and the flashes of gunfire."

"Where did they all come from?" Tudway asked. "Where did Cain get all those men?"

"Beats the hell out of me. I thought he was a loner," Dudley said.

"Where's Pauley?" Tudway asked.

"He's out there somewhere."

"What's he doing out there?" Tudway demanded. "He should be in here, protecting me. That's what I pay him for."

"He is protectin' you, Mr. Tudway," Austin said. "That's why he's out there."

"You two men, don't you go out there," Tudway ordered. "You stay in here with me, do you hear me? You make sure nobody gets in here."

"Don't you worry about that, Mr. Tudway. I got no intention of goin' out there."

At that moment a bullet crashed through the front window, whistled across the room, and thocked into the wall on the opposite side.

"Damn! Did you see that?" Dudley asked.

"Get down," Austin said. "We could get our fool heads shot off in here, just by standin' in front of the window like this."

As if to emphasize his statement, another bullet crashed through another window. Both men dropped to the floor, all the while keeping a sharp eye outside. Tudway was already lying on the floor.

With all three of them on the floor and looking through the front windows, Lucas was able to move from the door of the back room, across the open area of the parlor, to the foot of the stairs. At that point he would be no more than ten feet away from Tudway, but as there were no lanterns lit inside the house, the only light came from the burning barn, and that left enough dark shadows that Lucas felt his chances were pretty good.

Slowly, cautiously, he started up the stairs. The first step creaked, and Lucas came to a dead stop.

"What was that?" Tudway asked.

"What was what? I didn't hear nothin'," Dudley said.

"That...that creaking sound," Tudway said. "You didn't hear it?"

Lucas remained absolutely motionless.

"I didn't hear nothin'," Dudley said again. "Did you, Austin?"

"No," Austin answered.

Part of the barn caved in with a loud creaking crash.

"I heard that," Austin said.

"Yeah," Tudway said. "That must've been what I heard too."

Lucas waited until all three were looking out through the windows again, then he started up the stairs. Fortunately, only the first step was loose, and he was able to climb the rest of them without another sound.

Suddenly the firing stopped, and it grew silent outside. Then Lucas could hear Pauley's voice.

"Quit shootin'! Quit your firin'! You're shootin' at your own people!"

"We got some people hurt!"

"Let's have some help over here!"

Lucas listened to the men shout at each other outside while he continued to move quietly along the wall of the upstairs hallway. He stopped just before he reached the open door of the first room. He knew from his earlier observation that there was someone in this room. Lucas placed his back against the wall alongside the open door, then reached over and tapped lightly on the door frame.

"Yeah?" a voice called from inside.

Lucas tapped again.

"What do you want?"

Lucas tapped again.

"Dammit, I said what do you want?" the voice from inside said. Lucas heard him get up from the window and walk across the room. Lucas waited until he was right at the door, then stepped around the corner and hit him with a good, solid blow right on the point of the chin. The man went down like a sack of flour.

Lucas moved quickly on down the hallway until he reached the room where he knew from his earlier observation that he would find the boy. Slowly, he pushed the door open and looked inside. He saw a young boy with black hair and dark eyes sitting on the floor. The young Mexican woman Lucas had seen drawing a bucket of water the first day he arrived was crouched in a corner. As she looked at Lucas her large, black eyes were wide. Strangely, Lucas thought, the girl's eyes seemed to be reflecting more curiosity than fear.

Lucas put his finger to his lips to quiet her, then he shook his head slowly to reassure her. "Don't be afraid," he said quietly. "I won't hurt you."

"I am not afraid, señor," the girl replied in a quiet, steady voice.

Lucas held his hand out toward the small boy. "*Vamanos*, Roberto, I will take you to your papa," he said.

The boy looked at the young woman who had been with him, and she nodded. He didn't move when Lucas picked him up. With a nod of thanks to the young woman, Lucas backed out of the room and started back down the hall. He stepped over the man he had knocked unconscious and moved to the head of the stairs. Halfway down the stairs, a lantern was suddenly lit in the parlor. Lucas stopped in his tracks. Though the lantern didn't throw enough light up the stairs to expose him immediately, it did make everything brighter, and it meant he would have to pass through a patch of light before he could sneak out the back.

Someone came in through the front door, and Lucas had to wait, for he knew that whoever had just come in would be in a position to see him when he reached the bottom of the stairs. He also knew that the man he knocked out upstairs wouldn't be out much longer. He couldn't stay here and he couldn't go on.

"What the hell was all that about out there, Pauley?" Lucas heard Tudway ask.

"The men you sent out after Cain came back," Pauley said. "When they did, the men here started shootin' at them."

"That was a damn fool thing to do."

"It's dark out there," Pauley said. "You can't see your hand in front of your face."

"That's no excuse to be shootin' up your own men," Tudway said.

"It is if you ain't got nothin' but a bunch of cowhands that ain't ever fired a pistol at nothin' more'n a rattler before," Pauley said. "I told you not to send them out. They didn't do nothin' but get in the way."

"And I told you I want Lucas Cain and I don't care how I get him," Tudway replied. "How many did we get hurt out there?"

"Four, near as I can figure," Pauley answered. "And two more was killed."

"Four hurt? Austin, you and Dudley get out there and see if you can help," Tudway said. The two men left, then Tudway turned back to Pauley. "Who got killed?"

"Hatten and Findley. And Pork will probably die. He's gut-shot pretty bad."

"Too bad. Pork's a good man."

"Yeah, Pork's a good man. Hatten and Findley was

good men—hell, they're all good men," Pauley said. "Only thing is, good men ain't good enough for somebody like Lucas Cain. If you're serious about killing him, Mr. Tudway, you're goin' to have to let me do it my way. No more cowboys, no more ranch hands. I just want the men I've picked."

"All right, all right," Tudway said. "Have it your way. Only get him."

Tudway and Pauley turned back toward the window to look outside. That was what Lucas was waiting for, so he moved out of the shadow and down the stairs, intending to slip out through the back door. When he reached the bottom step, however, Roberto suddenly stuck his hand out toward Tudway.

"Grandpa," Roberto said.

"Roberto, what are you doing down here?" Tudway asked as he turned around. When he saw Lucas, he gasped. "You!"

Pauley turned too. Lucas had the advantage over both of them because he had his pistol in his hand. Tudway and Pauley's guns were in their holsters.

Pauley smiled at Lucas.

"Hello, Lucas. I figured you'd get here sooner or later," he said.

"Grandpa?" Roberto said again. He began wriggling in Lucas's arms reaching out toward Tudway.

"Hold still," Lucas said.

"Put the boy down, Cain," Tudway said. "Can't you see he wants to come to his grandpa?"

"You're his grandpa?" Lucas asked, surprised by the unexpected turn.

"That's right," Tudway said. "Oh," he headed, smiling broadly. "You mean you didn't *know* I was the boy's grandfather? Well, that's not surprising. I don't suppose

Leah wanted you to know that. So you see, you went through all this trouble for nothing. The boy belongs here as much as he does at Davenport Court."

"It doesn't matter," Lucas said. "I'm getting paid to take the boy back to Mrs. Davenport, and that's what I'm going to do. Take your guns out—slowly."

"Lucas, there are almost thirty men out there," Pauley reminded him. "And they're getting paid to see that you *don't* take the kid back. Do you really think you're going to make it out of here?"

"I'm going to try," Lucas said.

"Look. Maybe we can work something out," Tudway said. "You leave the kid here, I'll let you get out alive."

"Now, you wouldn't really want to let me walk out of here, Mr. Tudway," Lucas said. "You know I'd just come back."

"Yeah," Tudway said. "I guess you're right. All right, go ahead, Cain, try it. See how far you get."

There was an almost imperceptible change in Tudway's voice. Lucas wasn't exactly sure what it was, but it was as if the situation was reversed, as if Tudway were holding the gun on him. Suddenly the hair on the back of Lucas's neck prickled, and he turned just as the butt end of a pistol came down hard on his head.

17

When Lucas came to, he was in a dark room. The top of his head throbbed with pain, and for a moment he didn't know where he was or why his head was hurting. Then he remembered seeing Gus just as Gus brought his gun crashing down on his head, and he knew what had happened.

At about the same time Lucas remembered what had happened to him, he also realized that his hands and feet were tied. He wasn't tied down to the table where he was lying, so he sat up and swung his legs over the edge of the table.

The effort of sitting up made him so dizzy that he nearly fell back down again. He had to wait for several moments before the dizziness and nausea passed. When it finally went away, he managed to push himself off the table, and this time he had no trouble with maintaining his balance.

The only way Lucas could move was to hop around. But at least, he thought, he could do that. That was much better than not being able to do anything at all. Using the hopping motion, he began to explore the room that was his prison. The exploration was made even more difficult by the fact that it was so dark that he couldn't see six inches in front of his face. Several times he hopped into an obstruction, banging himself painfully, but he continued his exploration.

On one wall he found a shelf that held several wooden barrels. Lucas leaned over to take a sniff of one of the barrels and caught the distinctive odor of coal oil. He felt around with his hands until he located the petcock, and when he twisted it, he was rewarded with a small trickle.

Lucas held his hands under the trickle, letting the coal oil run onto the rope with which he was bound. When enough of it was soaked up, he hopped away from the barrel, then felt in his shirt pocket for his makings. He smiled when he discovered that they had not taken his little waterproof pouch of tobacco, paper, and, more importantly, matches.

Lucas pulled a match out, lit it, then set fire to the rope that bound his wrists. The flame billowed up, not only burning the ropes, but painfully searing his flesh. He gritted his teeth to keep from crying out and put as much pressure against the ropes as he could. Finally one of the ropes parted and Lucas's hands were free.

The burning rope fell to the floor, now providing him with a secondary advantage. By the light of the burning rope, he could not only see to free his feet, he could also take a look around the room where he was being kept.

Lucas rubbed his wrists gingerly as he explored his prison. He could see now that he was in the cellar of the big house. He found the door, but as it was made of heavy oak and bound with iron, there was little chance he would be able to break through it. There were several windows around but they were narrow slits between the bottom of the house and the top of the ground, much too small for him to wriggle through. As the last flicker of flame died out Lucas looked up to see the bottom of the floor of the big house. The floor was braced with heavy timbers and cross beams. Reaching up to grab one of the beams, he pulled himself up. He hung there for a moment, then dropped back down and waited.

Gradually the darkness rolled away as a gray, morning light began seeping in through the little window slits. When the light was bright enough that Lucas could see every corner of the room, he heard someone coming down the stairs. Quickly, he moved over to the door, then reached overhead and pulled himself up into the cross braces. He held himself in position, seven feet above the floor, as the door opened.

"Come along, Cain. Mr. Tudway has plans for you this morning," a man said as he rattled a key in the door lock. Lucas recognized the voice as belonging to Gus.

Gus pushed the door open and stepped inside.

"Come on," he called. "We don't want to keep Mr. Tudway waiting, do—what the hell?" he shouted suddenly.

At that moment, Lucas dropped down to the floor just behind Gus. Gus tried to turn around, but before he could do so, Lucas put one hand on the back of his neck and another at his belt. Lucas then gave him what was known as the "bums' rush" across the cellar floor, headed for the wooden coal oil barrels. Just before they reached the barrels, he forced Gus's head down. Then using his head like a battering ram, Lucas thrust Gus's head right through the end of the barrel and into thirty-five gallons of suffocating coal oil.

Gus flailed and struggled, but Lucas held him down,

keeping his head inside like holding him under water, only instead of water, it was coal oil. Gus's struggles grew weaker and weaker until finally they stopped altogether. Lucas pulled him out and dropped him to the floor. As Gus's head came out a flood of coal oil spilled out of the damaged barrel.

Gus's eyes were open but opaque, and his face was blue. He wasn't breathing, and when Lucas felt his neck, there wasn't a pulse.

Lucas took Gus's gun belt and put it on. He pulled the pistol, then spun the cylinder to check the loads. After that, he opened the petcocks on the other barrels so that four streams of coal oil spilled to the floor.

Just as Lucas left the cellar he struck another match, lit it, and tossed it back inside. The match landed in a pool of coal oil and flamed up. Within seconds, the cellar room was a roaring inferno.

Lucas hurried up the stairs. The cellar door opened outside the house, and from there it was an easy dash to the river. Lucas could go downriver and be quite a distance away from the house before anyone noticed the fire or that he was gone. But he had no intention of doing that. He had come for the boy, and he wasn't going to leave without him.

"Hey!" Lucas heard someone shout just as he slipped out the cellar door. "Hey, look! The big house is on fire!"

"Fire! Fire! Get the buckets!" someone else yelled.

Staying close to the wall, Lucas moved around the corner of the house to the north side toward Roberto's room. Facing away from the bunkhouse and the foreman's house, he knew there was less chance he would be noticed here.

Lucas moved quickly from the corner of the house to the base of the cottonwood tree. Yesterday when he was casing the defenses of the house, he had noticed that there was a firing platform built in the tree at about the same level as the window of the boy's room. He decided to take a chance that since he had been captured, the guard who had been here yesterday would be gone today.

"Austin, is that you?" someone called down from the tree.

Lucas froze. Why was someone up there now? Then he realized that Pauley was a thorough man who covered every possibility. If Pauley was hired to keep anyone from getting the boy, he would probably keep someone there all the time.

"Yeah," Lucas grunted.

"What the hell is goin' on? Did someone yell fire?"

Lucas didn't answer. Instead he continued to climb the tree.

"If that damn house is on fire, I ain't plannin' on hangin' around in this tree," the guard said.

Lucas was almost to the platform.

"What are you comin' up here now for? There's near another hour before you relieve me," the guard said. He moved over to the edge of the platform and looked down just as Lucas reached that level. "What the hell? You ain't Austin!" the guard shouted.

The guard went for his gun. That was a mistake; he should have backed away from the edge, because while he was going for his gun, Lucas managed to grab his leg and jerk. The guard let out a startled shout of fear, then pitched forward, falling headfirst. Lucas looked down and saw the man's body lying grotesquely twisted on the ground below.

From the firing platform in the cottonwood tree it was an easy stretch to the window that led into Roberto's room. The window was closed, but even before he reached it, it slid up. Lucas jerked back with his gun in his hand, but the face that appeared in the window was that of the pretty young Mexican woman.

"Wait," she said. "I will hand the boy to you."

"Tell him to be quiet," Lucas said.

"He will not betray you again," the señorita said. "I told him you are a good man. You will take him to his papa."

The young woman handed Roberto to Lucas. Roberto, frightened by the height, wrapped his arms tightly around Lucas's neck. Lucas sat him on the platform.

"Wait while I help the señorita," Lucas said. The first signs of smoke were beginning to creep into the boy's room. "Come, quickly," Lucas said to the girl. "You have to get out of there. The house is on fire."

The young woman climbed onto the windowsill and reached out for Lucas. Like Roberto, she wrapped her arms around his neck as he swung her across. Then when all three of them were on the platform, Lucas helped them climb down.

"You ride a horse?" Lucas asked the girl.

"*Si señor*," she answered. "I am a very good rider."

"You're going to have a chance to prove it. I'm going to take you out of here with the boy and me," he said. "I don't think Tudway will treat you too kindly when he finds the boy gone. Besides, I think it might be easier for the boy if you come along too. Come on, let's get over to the corral."

As they moved away from the house they could hear a great deal of commotion going on behind them. By now the flames had broken out of the cellar and were beginning to leap up the side of the house. A bucket brigade was in place, but it was already obvious that they were fighting a losing battle.

The corral gate was halfway between the bunkhouse and what was left of the barn. The barn was only a pile of charred wood, totally destroyed in the fire last night. The fence of the corral was lined with all the saddles that had been saved from the fire. Lucas was just reaching for one when they heard someone coming from the other side of the bunkhouse. Lucas looked around quickly for someplace to hide, but there was no place.

"Señor!" the young woman shouted. "Here!" She lifted her full, brightly colored skirt and spread her legs.

Lucas smiled. He had heard of hiding *behind* a woman's skirt before. He had never heard of hiding *under* one. He slipped in between her legs, and she quickly put the skirt back down, then squeezed her bare legs against the side of his face. He could feel the twitching muscles in her legs.

"What are you and the boy doing out here?" Lucas heard someone ask.

"The house," the girl said. "It is on fire."

"I know it's on fire, girl. Hell, I can see that. But Tudway don't want that boy out of his sight."

"We will be safe here," the girl said.

"Maybe you'd better come on up here with us."

"Let her alone," the other man said. "She and the boy are out of the way here."

"Yeah, I guess you're right. Come on, we'd better get up there and help them with that fire before Tudway has a fit."

Lucas heard them walk away. A moment later, the girl raised her skirt.

"It is safe now, señor," she said.

"*Gracias*," Lucas said. He picked up the saddle. "Keep a

sharp eye out," he said. "I'll get us a couple of horses saddled and we'll get out of here."

As Lucas saddled the horses he debated in his mind whether or not he should scatter the rest of the horses. If he scattered them, it would take Tudway's men a while to round them back up and come after him. But they might hear the horses leaving and would know at once that he, the boy, and the girl watching him were getting away.

On the other hand, if he just left quietly, they would have a good lead on everyone before his absence was even discovered. As far as they knew, he was still trapped in the cellar. He decided that his best bet would be to just slip away as silently as he could.

Putting his finger to his lips to caution Roberto and the girl to be quiet, Lucas helped them into the saddle of one horse, then he mounted another. Slowly, quietly, they slipped away.

18

The girl's name was Cristina. She told Lucas she had come to Winning Hand with her mother five years ago. Her mother, who died last year, had been a cook and housekeeper for Jules Tudway. Cristina had not wanted to stay on at Winning Hand, she didn't like Jules Tudway and she was afraid of the hands, but there was no way she could leave until Lucas came along and offered her a way to escape. She was very grateful to him, she said, that he was taking her with him.

At first, Lucas thought Cristina would slow him down. But he quickly learned that she was not only as good a rider as she said she was, she was smart, resourceful, and whipcord tough. Once, when Winning Hand riders nearly found them, it was she who discovered the ravine they hid in. They moved their horses quickly out of the way, then stayed there, bent low so as not to be seen. Cristina made tiny shushing, comforting noises to Roberto to keep him quiet.

They rode for the rest of the day in heat so fierce that

what little wind did stir, blew against their faces like a breath from the mouth of a furnace, but never once did she or the boy complain. The land unfolded before them in an endless vista of rocks, dirt, cactus, and mesquite. The sun heated the ground, sending up undulating waves, which caused near objects to shimmer and nonexistent lakes to appear tantalizingly in the distance.

Normally it was one hard day's ride from Winning Hand into Tudway. It would be longer now, because Lucas wasn't going by the most direct route. He was taking a circuitous path because he hoped to avoid an ambush. That proved to be a vain hope, however, when a pistol cracked and a bullet whizzed by, taking his hat off, fluffing his hair, and sending shivers down his spine.

"Get down!" Lucas shouted at Cristina, but his warning was unnecessary, for in one motion she had already grabbed the boy and hit the ground, diving behind a low bank of rocks about twenty feet to Lucas's left.

Lucas was down at about the same time, slapping the horses on the flank to get them out of the line of fire. He too dived for the protection of a little clump of rocks just as a second shot came so close to his ear he could hear the air pop as the bullet sped by.

Lucas wriggled his body to the end of the little bank of rocks, then peered around cautiously. Though he couldn't see anybody, he did see the signature of a presence, a little puff of smoke from the rifle shot. The smoke was drifting north on a hot breath of air. That meant that the shooter was somewhat to the south, so Lucas moved his eyes in that direction. He saw the tip of a hat rising slowly above the rocks and he figured the shooter was raising up to take another shot.

Lucas watched as the hat began to move up, and he cocked his pistol and waited. When enough of the hat was visible to provide a good target, Lucas aimed and fired. The hat went sailing away.

"Ha! That's an old trick, Cain!" a voice called. "I had my hat on the end of a stick."

Lucas fired again, this time at the sound of the voice. His bullet set chips of rock flying and he was rewarded with a yelp of pain.

"You son of a bitch! You sprayed rock into my face," the shooter said.

"Sorry," Lucas replied. "I was trying to put a bullet in your forehead."

The shooter chuckled. "Yeah," he said. "I'll just bet you were."

"Who are you?" Lucas asked.

"Why do you need to know?"

"No reason. I just like to know the names of the people I kill," Lucas said.

"Or the name of the man that's going to kill you?"

"That too," Lucas agreed.

"The name is LaRoche. Dodd LaRoche. Ever heard of me?"

"Yeah," Lucas said. "Yeah, I have. I didn't know you were working for Tudway."

"I wasn't," LaRoche said. "Not until this mornin'. He sent me a letter about a week or so back offerin' me a job. I just come onto the place this mornin', right after your little fracas there and just in time to join in the little fox hunt and get in on the reward."

"What reward?"

"What reward? Why, mister, there's a five-thousand-dollar price tag on your head. Did you know that?"

"I never knew I was so valuable."

Unexpectedly, LaRoche chuckled. "Well, it ain't hard to figure out why. You got to be a burr in Tudway's saddle real fast. You already killed what, ten of his men? Plus, you destroyed his granary, cookhouse, barn, and you burned down the big house. Why, General Sherman hisself didn't do as much damage to Georgia as you already done to Winning Hand Ranch."

"It could've been avoided," Lucas said. "All Tudway had to do was let me have the boy and I would've left."

"Yeah, well, things don't always work out like they're planned, do they?" LaRoche said. "Like you take now for instance. Here you thought you was goin' to make a clean getaway. But I had me a notion you might go this way, so I got out here before you. Pretty smart of me, don't you think? This is like money in the bank."

"LaRoche, have you ever heard the old saying 'don't count your chickens before they hatch'?"

"Yeah, I've heard it. What about it?"

"Well, I ain't hatched," Lucas said.

"Maybe not, but you ain't for from it," LaRoche said.

Suddenly the boy cried out and Lucas heard Cristina's voice, tinged with fear. "Señor Cain!" she shouted. "I got 'em, Dodd! I got 'em!" a man's voice shouted. It was the first time Lucas realized that there was more than one person facing him.

"Good job, Elroy," LaRoche said.

"Cristina? Roberto?" Lucas called. "Are you all right?"

"Don't you worry none about them, Cain, they're just fine," the new voice said. "I'm takin' good care of 'em."

"Stand up, Cain," Dodd LaRoche called. "Stand up, or we'll kill the woman and the kid."

Lucas looked over and saw that Cristina and Roberto were already standing. Slowly, reluctantly,

Lucas stood up, holding his hands up. His pistol was in one hand.

"Well, now," Dodd LaRoche said. He stood up from his position behind a rock about thirty yards away from Lucas. He was pointing a gun at Lucas and smiling. "Stand up, Elroy," he said. "Let the big man here get a good look at the two men who are about to kill him."

When Elroy stood up, Lucas saw that he was right behind Cristina and Roberto. Roberto was standing close to Cristina, with his arms wrapped around her leg and almost enveloped in her red and yellow skirt. Roberto was looking on at the scene with fear-enlarged eyes.

"Oh, by the way," Dodd added. "You said you liked to know all the names of the folks you did business with, allow me to introduce you to this gentleman. This here is Elroy."

"Elroy," Lucas said. "Would you be Elroy Wright?" he asked.

"Yeah, Elroy Wright. You mean you heard of me?" Wright asked.

"I've seen paper on you."

Wright giggled. "Well now, what do you think about that, Dodd? Cain has heard of me. I got a famous marshal chasin' after me."

"I didn't say I was after you, Wright. I said I had seen reward circulars on you. You're nothing but a two-bit punk. There's not enough money on you to make you worth my time."

"Yeah?" Wright said angrily. "Well, we'll just see who's worth whose time. Throw down your gun, Cain."

"Wait," Dodd said. "Empty it first. I've heard tell that you was just a barrel of tricks. I don't want you to throw it down, then somehow drop to your knees or somethin' and get a hold of it real quick. I think it would be better if you would take out the bullets first."

"Yeah," Elroy agreed. "Empty your gun, Cain."

Lucas punched two shells out of the revolver, then rolled the cylinder back two clicks, exposing two empty chambers. He dropped the bullets to the ground one at a time.

"Is that it? Two bullets?" LaRoche asked. "I said empty it."

"That's all I had left," Lucas said. "I had to steal this gun when I got away."

"I don't care if you had to make it. I don't believe the gun is empty," LaRoche said.

Lucas put the gun to his right temple and, staring impassively at LaRoche, pulled the trigger. The hammer fell with a dull, metallic click on an empty chamber.

"All right, it's empty," Elroy said. "Now put your gun down."

"Wait a minute, Elroy. I ain't ready for him to do it just yet," LaRoche put in. "I'd like to see you do that again, Cain," he said. "Pull the trigger one more time."

"Yeah." Elroy giggled. "Let us see you do it one more time."

Lucas looked over at Cristina and saw the anxious look on her face, as if she was about to witness a thing of horror.

"No, *Señor* Cain," she cried out. "Don't do it!"

Lucas hesitated for just a second, then pulled the trigger again. Again, there was a dull, metallic click as the hammer fell on an empty chamber.

LaRoche chuckled. "Damn, I was hopin' you were tryin' to trick me," he said. "I kinda wanted to see you blow your own brains out." Relaxed now, he lowered his pistol slightly.

That was the opening Lucas was looking for. He had rolled the cylinder back to provide for the two empty chambers. Now he had two loads ready and he jerked the pistol down from his temple and shot LaRoche in the heart, all in the same fluid motion.

"Look out!" Elroy screamed, trying to bring his own pistol around to aim at Lucas. As LaRoche was going down Lucas turned toward Elroy to fire his second shot, but a second shot wasn't needed. Before he could even shoot, Elroy dropped his gun and put his hands up to his throat to try and stop a fountain of blood pouring through his fingers. In the split-second Lucas was turning, he saw a blur and flash of red and yellow as Cristina whirled around and sent her hand to Elroy's throat, made one quick slashing motion, then pulled her hand away. The blade of the knife she was holding was already red with Elroy's blood.

Elroy pitched forward, flopped a couple of times like a fish out of water, then died with a life-surrendering gurgle.

"Are you all right?" Lucas asked.

"*Si*."

"Where did you learn a trick like that?"

"Before my mother and I came to Winning Hand, we lived with my father's people," Cristina said.

"Who were they?"

"Apache, señor," she said easily.

"Yeah? I know the Apache. They're good people to have on your side," Lucas said. He began reloading the pistol. "Pick up the kid. I'll get the horses."

They rode until dark, then made a cold camp. The camp was not only cold, it was hungry. The little supply of beef jerky that Lucas normally carried was in the saddlebag of his own horse, and he had no idea where his own horse was.

Shortly after they made camp, Cristina disappeared. Lucas didn't question her, thinking she might have some personal business to take care of, but when she returned a few moments later, he saw that she had a shawl full of cactus pears. Using her knife and disregarding the needles and spines that had already pricked her skin so many times that her hands were streaked with blood, Cristina peeled the pears, then parceled the sweet fruit out among the three of them.

Later that night, with Roberto asleep, Lucas lay with his head on his saddle, looking up at the starry vault overhead.

"Señor Cain," Cristina said. "Do you think I am pretty?"

Lucas raised up on one elbow and looked over at her. She was lying on her back, looking up at the stars.

"Sure," he said. "I think you are a very pretty woman."

"And will other men think this?"

"Well, of course they would," Lucas replied.

"Roberto's papa. Do you think he will find me pretty?"

Lucas smiled. So this was where she was going with her questions.

"I don't know Carlos Ortiz," Lucas admitted. "But I think he would have to be blind not to appreciate you."

"It is my wish that he would find me pretty," Cristina said. "I would like to become his wife. If he thinks I am pretty, when I asked him to marry with me, he will say yes."

"Wait a minute, hold on here," Lucas said. "You don't want to do that."

"No?"

"No."

"Why not? Is Señor Ortiz not a good man?"

"Well, yes, he's a good man, all right. That is, I'm sure he is a good man, or Mrs. Davenport wouldn't keep him around," Lucas said. "But that's not what I'm talking about. What I mean is, you shouldn't go around asking a man to marry you."

"But why not? I wish to be married. I do not want to become a . . . what do the Americans call an old woman who is not married?"

"An old maid."

"Yes, I do not wish to become an old maid."

Lucas chuckled. "I don't think you're going to have to worry about that," he said. "Anyway, it isn't right for a woman to ask a man. The man should do the asking."

"But Roberto's papa does not know me," Cristina said. "How can he ask me?"

"I don't know," Lucas replied.

"Then is it not foolish for me to wait for him to ask?"

"There are ways to make him ask you," Lucas said.

"How?"

"How? I don't know that, either. I just know that there are ways…women's ways," Lucas said, trying to explain it to her.

"But if I do not know this woman's way, and if you do not know how to tell me, how can I make Roberto's papa marry with me?"

"Maybe Mrs. Davenport can help you," Lucas said. "She'll know how it's done."

"Will you ask Mrs. Davenport to teach me how to make Roberto's papa want to marry with me?"

"Yes," Lucas said. "I will ask."

"*Gracias.* You are a good man, Señor Cain. If I did not

already have my heart set to marry with Roberto's papa, I would want to marry with you."

Lucas smiled and thought, Thank God for Roberto's papa. But what he said was, "Good night, Cristina."

"Good night, *Señor* Cain."

THE FIRST PINK fingers of dawn touched the cactus, and the light was soft and the air was cool. Lucas liked the range best early in the morning and he watched as the last morning star made a bright pinpoint of light over the purple mountains lying in a ragged line far to the west.

He had not built a fire this morning because he didn't want to take a chance on the smoke being seen. He didn't really need a fire anyway. He had no coffee to brew, no bacon to cook, no biscuits to bake. He could do without the bacon and biscuits but he really wished he had a cup of coffee.

A rustle of wind through feathers caused him to look up just in time to see a golden eagle diving on its prey. The eagle swooped back into the air carrying a tiny field mouse, kicking fearfully in the eagle's claws. A Gila monster scurried beneath a nearby mesquite tree, which was itself dying under the burden of parasitic mistletoe.

Lucas took a deep breath to enjoy these last few moments alone, then he walked over to wake Cristina.

"Time to go," he said. "Get the boy ready. I'll saddle the horses."

"The place we are going," Cristina said. "Will we reach it soon?"

"Today," Lucas said. "We will reach it today."

Lucas saddled the horses as Cristina roused Roberto

from his sleep. He thought about what was in front of them. He had lied to Cristina when he said they would reach Tudway today. In fact, if they went in a straight line, they could be there in just a few hours. And he believed now that they couldn't go in a straight line if they wanted to, because he knew that the Winning Hand men were no longer waiting for them out on the range. He was sure they were already in Tudway, waiting for him there. For that reason, Lucas decided that they wouldn't actually enter the town until after dark.

19

The night creatures raised their songs to the stars as Lucas, Cristina, and Roberto approached Tudway. A cloud passed over the moon, then moved away, bathing the little town that rose from the prairie before them in silver. Some of the buildings were dark, though most showed varying degrees of illumination, from the dull glow of a single lantern or candle to the brightness created by dozens of lamps. The most brightly lit buildings were the saloons.

Like the creatures of the prairie, the town dwellers had their own brand of night music. As Lucas approached the little community, he could hear the orchestral change. The soft hoot of owls, the trilling songs of frogs, and the distant howls of coyotes gave way to tinkering pianos, off-key singing, clinking glasses, and an occasional outburst of laughter.

Lucas looked toward the depot and saw that Mrs. Davenport's car was brightly lighted.

Lucas was about to move toward the car when a shadow passed in front of one of the car windows. That meant there were people outside, around the car. Lucas had noticed them before, so now he stopped and examined the car more closely. In examining the car, Lucas used a trick of night vision that he had learned from the time he had spent with the Indians. He had been taught that staring directly at something in the dark would make it disappear, though he had no idea why that was so. He also didn't understand why looking to one side of the object would sometimes make the object pop right into view. All he knew was that the trick worked. Using that technique of nighttime observation, Lucas soon saw that there were at least four men guarding Mrs. Davenport's private car. That meant that the Winning Hand men were already in town. Lucas wasn't surprised that they were here before him. They would have had the advantage of being able to come straight to town, whereas it had been necessary for him to take a more circuitous route in order to evade his pursuers.

"I'm sure those are Winning Hand men down there," Lucas said with a disgusted sigh. He pointed to the car. "At least four men are guarding Mrs. Davenport's car. That probably means that Pauley, and maybe Tudway, are in town."

"I see many more Winning Hand men there, *señor*," Cristina said, pointing toward the Golden Eagle Saloon.

"Yeah," Lucas said. "Well, knowing Pauley, he isn't likely to leave anything uncovered. I'm sure he has men in both saloons, the restaurant, all the stores, and all over town."

"What do we do now, Señor Cain?" Cristina asked.

"I don't know just yet," Lucas said. "But I'm going to have to think of something."

Roberto was sitting in the saddle in front of Cristina

and he twisted around and looked up toward her. "Cristina, I'm hungry," he said.

"Shh, my little one," Cristina replied. Tenderly she brushed the hair from his eyes.

Lucas watched the byplay between the two. "I don't blame the boy," he said. "I'm hungry too. We're going to have to go somewhere where we can get something to eat and find a place that the boy can rest."

"I know where we can go," Cristina said. "If you do not mind."

"Mind? Why should I mind? Listen, Cristina, if you have an idea, let's hear it." Lucas said.

"We can go there," Cristina said, pointing to the darker part of the town. This was the Mexican section and it was darker because only a few of the Mexican families could afford lanterns. Most of the homes had to depend on candles or burning pine knots for illumination. However, as in the American section of town. The most brightly lit building was the saloon, or cantina, and it was to the cantina that Cristina actually pointed. "None of Señor Tudway's men will be in the Mexican cantina."

"Yeah," Lucas agreed. "Yeah, that's a good idea. All right, let's go."

Lucas and Cristina rode in a wide circle around Tudway in order to come into town on the Mexican side. As they drew closer to the cantina, Lucas could hear someone playing a guitar. The guitarist was very good and the music spilled out in a steady beat with two or three poignant minor chords at the end of each phrase. And overall, the single-string melody worked its way in and out of the chords like a thread of gold woven through the finest cloth. Lucas liked that kind of music. It was mournful, lonesome music, the kind of melody a man could let run through his mind during long, quiet rides.

Lucas caught the smell of beans and spicy beef coming from the cantina, and because it had been several days now since he had eaten well, his stomach growled in protest. A barking dog ran out to greet them, followed them for a few feet with its sharp yapping, then satisfied that it had successfully defended its territory, fell off and return to its owner's house.

By the time they reached the front of the cantina the music had stopped, so that the only sound coming from inside was conversation. Lucas was gratified to hear that the language being spoken was Spanish. He knew that few Americans came to this part of town, just as few Mexicans visited the American side. That should help keep news of his arrival from Tudway.

As they stepped into the lantern light that spilled through the front door they saw an old Mexican sitting in a chair, leaning back against the wall. The Mexican was wearing a high-crowned, wide-brimmed sombrero and a fringed serape. Lucas was sure that the serape was brightly colored, though the colors were muted in the dim light.

"*Buenas noches,*" the old man greeted.

"*Buenas noches, señor,*" Lucas said.

"*Americano?*" the old man asked.

"*Si,*" Lucas answered. "*Nosotros desear a comer.*"

"*Que?*" the old man asked, clearly not understanding Lucas's attempt at Spanish.

Cristina laughed. "He does not understand what you are trying to say," she said.

"Tell him we wish to eat."

"Ah, you wish to eat! Yes!" the Mexican said, having overheard Lucas's words to Cristina. "Why did you not say so? You do not need to speak to me in Spanish. I can speak English very good. My name is Fernando Rodriguez. Everyone will tell you, Fernando Rodriguez speaks English very good. Do you not think so?"

"Yes, I congratulate you on your fine skill," Lucas said. "We have come a long way, Fernando, without food and with very little water. And as you can see, we have a young child with us. Can you tell us where might be a good place to eat?"

"But you can eat inside, señor," Fernando said, standing and bowing, and motioning to the door with a sweep of his hat. "My wife is the cook in this place. She makes the best *frijoles* you will ever eat. Please, you must try them."

"*Gracias*," Lucas said. "I will try them."

As advertised, Señora Rodriguez's *frijoles* were about the best Lucas had ever tasted, though he was fully aware that hunger was, in the final analysis, the best spice. He rolled a *tortilla* in his fingers and, using it like a spoon, scooped up the last of his second serving of the spicy beans. Cristina and Roberto had shown just as hearty an appetite.

By now the others in the bar already knew who he was, and Lucas had heard his name whispered in awe and fear at half a dozen tables. His sudden and unexpected arrival had become the center of everyone's conversation, replacing whatever intercourse had been taking place before he arrived. Everyone knew of the presence in town of the men from Winning Hand Ranch, and all knew that they were here to kill Lucas Cain. But Cristina, addressing everyone in Spanish, had appealed to them to keep secret the fact that Lucas was here. And, as Cristina explained to Lucas, since nearly every Mexican in Tudway had his own grievance against Jules Tudway, it was a pretty sure thing that their secret would be safe.

"Now that we are here, what do we do next?" Cristina asked. "We can't stay here forever. And how will you deliver Roberto to Mrs. Davenport and to his father?"

"I've been thinking about that little problem," Lucas said, washing down the beans with a cup of strong coffee. "And I may have an answer to it if I can get *Señor* Rodriguez to help us."

"I will ask him to come speak with you," Cristina said, going back out front where Fernando had reclaimed his chair.

A moment later Fernando, holding his sombrero in his hand, stood at Lucas's table.

"*Si, señor?* You wish to speak with Fernando Rodriguez?"

"Yes," Lucas replied. "Tell me, Señor Rodriguez, is Tudway in town?"

"*Si.* He is in town," Rodriguez said.

"And Pauley? Is he in town?"

"*Si,*" Rodriguez said. "He is in town, too."

"Do you know *why* they are in town?"

"*Si,*" Rodriguez said. Quickly, he crossed himself. "They are here to kill you, señor."

"That's right," Lucas said. "But that's not going to happen if you help me."

"Me? But, señor, I know nothing about guns," Rodriguez said, his face reflecting fear over the idea of his having to be in a gun battle. "If you want me to fight for you, I will not be very good."

"No. It's nothing like that," Lucas said. "Do you know

the boy who works at Crawford's Livery Stable? His name is Billy Williams."

"Billy Williams," Fernando said. "*Si*, I know him."

"I want you to bring him here to see me," Lucas asked. "But I don't want any of the Americans to know about it."

"Señor Billy Williams is an *Americano*. I think he will not come to a Mexican cantina," Rodriguez said.

"He will come if he knows I've sent for him," Lucas replied. "And if you tell him I'm here and I need his help."

"Very well, *señor*. I will get him for you," Fernando said.

It was no more than fifteen minutes later when Lucas saw two Mexicans coming in through the front door. One was Fernando Rodriguez. Lucas chuckled when he realized that the other was Billy Williams. Fernando had taken an extra sombrero and serape with him when he went to see the boy, and using that, Billy was able to come into the Mexican part of town without arousing any curiosity.

Billy was smiling broadly when he sat down in the chair offered by Lucas.

"All of Tudway's men are sayin' you'll be shot dead the moment you set foot in town," Billy said. "I'm glad to see you was able to make a liar out of 'em"

"How many men does Tudway have in town?" Lucas asked.

"Oh, I couldn't give you an exact number," Billy said. "But they's a whole lot of 'em, that's for sure. Most of 'em are over in the Golden Eagle, talkin' about how they're goin' to spend the money they're goin' to get whenever you're kilt. There's quite a big reward on your head, did you know that, Mr. Cain?"

Lucas smiled across the table at Billy. "So I've heard. You aren't tempted by it, are you, Billy?"

"No, sir!" Billy gasped, shocked that Lucas would even suggest it. "Do you think I would turn you in for the reward money?"

Lucas laughed. "I was only teasing," he said. "I figured I could trust you; that's why I sent for you. Now, tell me about Pauley and Tudway. Fernando says they're both in town. Have you seen them?"

"Yes, sir."

"Where are they right now? Are they together?"

"No, sir, they ain't together. Pauley's down to the depot, keepin' a close eye on Mrs. Davenport's private railroad car. And Tudway, he's got hisself a private apartment overlooking the emporium." Billy laughed. "I reckon he's goin' to have to live there for a while, seein' as he don't have no house to stay in out on Winning Hand anymore. Folks are sayin' there ain't nothin' left out there now. They say you left it lookin' most like Atlanta after the siege."

"I like to leave a mark when I can," Lucas said.

Billy laughed, then he grew curious. "Rodriguez said you needed my help, Mr. Cain. What is it I can do for you?"

"Billy, I need to get Cristina and the boy down to Mrs. Davenport's car. After that, I need to get the car hooked on to the next train going east so I can get them out of town," Lucas said.

Billy shook his head. "Mr. Cain, there ain't no doubt in my mind that you are the best man in this town, by far. But even with me helpin' you, there would still only be two of us. And there's a whole army of them Winning Hand riders, ever'one of 'em itchin' to get their hands on that reward money Tudway's promised. No, sir, I don't see no way on God's green earth we'd make it even down to the depot, let alone out of town."

"Maybe we can even the odds out a bit," Lucas suggested.

"How are you goin' to do that?" Billy wanted to know.

"I got an idea," Lucas said. "But it depends on Tudway helping me."

Billy blinked in surprise. "I beg your pardon? Did you say you wanted Tudway to help you?"

"That's what I said."

"What makes you think Tudway is goin' to help you?"

"I'll show you," Lucas said. "But first, I have to get him out of that apartment and away from Pauley or any of his men."

"How are you goin' to do that?"

"That's where you come in," Lucas said. "Maybe the two of us could sneak up to his apartment, grab him, and bring him here."

"We'd have to tie and gag him to sneak him out of there," Billy said. "And we'd have to pass right in front of the saloon. Don't you think it might look a little strange if we was to be seen carrying Tudway across the street like that?"

"Yeah, I guess so," Lucas said. "But we have to come up with something."

"How about his horse?" Cristina suggested.

"What do you mean?"

"Señor Tudway has a very fine horse," she explained. "It is what is called an Arabian horse. And all the time, *Señor* Tudway is worried about it. He cares very much for that horse."

"Well, the girl's tellin' the truth, all right," Billy said. "Fact is, I have that horse in a special stall right now. Special stall, special food, you name it, anything special in the way of takin' care of a horse and Mr. Tudway wants it. Why, you'd think that horse was pure gold the way he dotes over it."

"His horse," Lucas said. He laughed. "Yes, that's how we'll get him. Thanks, Cristina."

JULES TUDWAY, wearing a dressing gown of wine-colored silk, sat alone at a table in his apartment dealing out imaginary poker hands. He took a drink of brandy from his snifter, then putting the snifter down, adroitly deposited an ace onto the hand he was dealing himself. The ace completed his hand, giving him a full house of aces and eights. Chuckling, he turned over the other three hands, though it wasn't necessary. He knew what cards he had dealt each hand.

Yes, sir, he thought. If he had to, he could still earn a comfortable living playing cards.

Of course, Jules Tudway didn't have to play cards anymore. As a result of his skill with the pasteboards he was already one of the wealthiest men in the state. He had come a long way from the days when people used to call him a "tinhorn" gambler. Now he traveled in such fine company that he knew the governor on a first-name basis. There were even some people urging him to stand for the next election.

Tudway wasn't likely to acquiesce to their wishes, though. He had no political or altruistic ambition. What he wanted was to become the biggest and most successful rancher in the state, and he had nearly accomplished that goal when he encountered Lucas Cain. Now his beautiful ranch was in ruins all because of one man. And one woman.

Tudway got up from the table and walked over to the upstairs window of his apartment. He looked down toward the depot and at the private car that belonged to Leah Davenport. She had been Leah Stephens when he first met her, recently from Virginia, and more recently widowed.

Leah, the widow.

Leah, the bar girl.

Leah, the whore.

Leah wasn't like any other whore Tudway had ever known, though. She was a very discriminating kind of whore. She would only lie with those men that she chose to lie with, and no amount of money could make her change her mind. Tudway knew that to be a fact because he had tried to get her to go with him, offering her ten times as much money as any other woman ever got. Despite his generous offer Leah steadfastly refused.

Leah's refusal had been like a slap in Tudway's face. He couldn't just walk away from it. The fact that she had refused him time and time again caused him to want her all the more. He became obsessed with her. Finally, when all else failed, he pushed his way into her room one night, overpowered her, stuffed rags into her mouth so she couldn't scream, tied her to her bed, and took her.

The next day, a battered and bruised Leah went to the police to try to bring charges of rape against Tudway. Despite the obvious evidence of her beating, the police informed her that she had no case. That was because a "woman of her avocation" could not be raped.

As a result of the night that the police said never took place, Leah Stephens became pregnant with Jules Tudway's child. When Tudway learned about her condition, he offered to marry her, to give the baby a home and a name.

"Your name?" Leah had replied in cold anger. "I would see the child a homeless waif before I gave it your name."

Her refusal even to let Tudway help her was the cruelest cut of all. Any desire he may have once had was replaced by an anger that festered and grew until it turned into a deep and abiding hate.

On the night she delivered, Leah hired guards to keep Tudway away. It was a little girl, but Leah refused to let Tudway even see her. Then, almost a year after the little girl was born, an English cattle rancher named Rowland Davenport left his ranch in Southwest Texas for a visit to San Francisco. For Davenport the trip to San Francisco was a combination of business and pleasure and part of the pleasure was playing cards.

Davenport got into a card game with Tudway. Tudway had Davenport nearly broken when Leah talked the rancher into walking away from the table without playing another hand to "try and win back his losses." Leah knew that he could never win, and her intrusion allowed Davenport to hang on to more than half his holdings. A short time later Leah and Rowland Davenport were married.

Tudway was sure that Leah had married Davenport just to spite him. But he could be equally as spiteful.

Until Leah married Davenport, Tudway had not intended to keep the land he had won. He planned to sell it back to Davenport, perhaps at one-half its actual value. In Tudway's mind that seemed like the sensible thing to do. After all, he certainly had no interest in the business of ranching. What he was interested in was cold cash. However, when he learned that Leah was planning to marry Davenport, he changed his mind. He saw an opportunity to break Leah by breaking her husband.

Now Davenport was dead. Leah was still around, though, and Tudway knew he wouldn't be completely satisfied until he had destroyed her as well. It was, he thought, a rather delicious piece of irony that one of the weapons he had chosen to use against her was Roberto Ortiz, her grandson. *Their* grandson.

It galled Tudway to think that his grandson was one-half Mexican. But then, since he never had anything to do with Roberto until he had his men snatch the boy, it didn't really make that much difference whether he was half Mexican or not. And it made it easier for him to do what he had to do. He felt no compunctions about snatching the boy and using him to force Leah Davenport to sell the springhead to him.

Of course, Tudway didn't actually have the boy right now. Lucas Cain had him, but Tudway wasn't particularly worried about that. He knew that there was no way Cain could get by Pauley and his men in order to deliver the child to Leah. And as long as Leah was denied her grandchild, Tudway was accomplishing the same thing.

A knock on the door interrupted Tudway's musings, and he turned away from the window.

"Yes?"

"Mr. Tudway, it's me, Billy Williams," a voice called from outside the door.

"Who?"

"Billy Williams, Mr. Tudway. You know, from Crawford's Livery Stable?"

"What do you want?"

"It's about your horse, Mr. Tudway."

Tudway opened the door and saw the young man

standing there, holding his hat in his hand, with a pained look on his face.

"What about my horse?" Tudway asks sharply.

"I don't know," Billy said. "There's something wrong with him. He's sick or something. I think maybe you'd better come down and take a look."

Tudway reached for his hat. "Boy, if you've done something to that horse, given him the wrong feed or something, you are going to answer to me. Do you understand me?"

"I didn't do nothin' wrong, Mr. Tudway," Billy said. "I just think you should come down and see him for yourself, that's all."

"Let's go," Tudway said, stepping outside and closing his apartment door behind him.

20

"There he is, Mr. Tudway," Billy said, pointing to the stall at the far end of the stable. "He's down there."

"What the hell is he doing down there?" Tudway asked. "I thought you were keeping him in the special stall."

"Yes, sir, I was. But I moved him down here when he started actin' up. I was afraid he might spook the other horses."

"You get him back where he belongs," Tudway said angrily as he opened the stall door and stepped inside. He reached for his horse but he never connected, for just at that moment, someone suddenly stood up from the shadows. By the way he was dressed, Tudway could tell that he was Mexican. "Who are you?" he demanded. "What are you doing in here with my horse?"

Another Mexican suddenly appeared, this time from behind Tudway. Tudway realized then that he was in danger, but before he could cry out, he was hit over the head with a blunt object. He went out like a light.

A moment later one of the Winning Hand riders happened to step through the front door of the Golden Eagle Saloon to get a little fresh air. When he did so, he saw two Mexicans coming out of the livery stable. They were carrying a third person, wrapped in a serape, with a sombrero placed over his face.

"Hey!" the Winning Hand rider called out. "If you Mex fellas can't hold your liquor, you ought not to be out!" He laughed at his own joke.

THE NIGHT PASSED without further incident.

At the crack of dawn, a rooster crowed.

Somewhere a back door opened, and a housewife came out carrying a bucket. She sat the bucket under the pump and began pumping water and the squeaking *clank, clank, clank* of the pump could be heard over most of the town.

A dog barked.

A baby cried.

Deke Pauley had slept the night on a wooden bench in the depot, and the morning sounds woke him up. He stood up, stretched, and scratched, then walked over to the edge of the platform where he relieved himself on the railroad tracks, making no attempt to preserve modesty. In the east, the sun was above the horizon, a blood-orange ball that had not yet picked up its heat and brilliance.

"Austin, Dudley," Pauley called and he buttoned his pants.

Dudley had been sleeping out on the depot platform, and at Pauley's call he got up. Austin was at that moment walking down the street toward the depot from downtown. He was carrying something, and when he got close enough, Pauley could see that it was a plate of biscuits and bacon. Pauley reached for one.

"You two fellas decide to sleep in this mornin'?" Austin teased. "I already been all over town. Got these down at the Chuckwagon."

"Anybody see any sign of Cain last night?" Pauley asked, taking a big bite.

"Not hide nor hair," Austin answered. "There's somethin' kind of strange goin' on, though."

"Strange? What do you mean, strange?"

"Well, it's Mr. Tudway. Nobody seems to know where he is."

"He's in his apartment over the emporium," Pauley said easily.

"No, he ain't," Austin said. "I done checked. He wasn't over at the Chuckwagon and he wasn't at the saloon either."

A piece of biscuit hung on Pauley's lip and he wiped it off before he spoke. "Well, what do you mean, dammit? He has to be somewhere. What's the storekeeper's name at the emporium? Felix Helman? Did you ask him?"

"Yeah, I did, and this is where it gets more strange. Helman says he heard the stable boy come get Tudway last night. They was talkin' somethin' about Tudway's horse. Anyway, Helman seen Tudway and the boy go down to the stable, but he never seen Tudway come back."

"Why didn't the son of a bitch say something about that last night?" Pauley demanded."

"He said he didn't think nothin' about it," Austin said.

"Get the stable boy," Pauley ordered. "Get him and bring him to me."

AT THE OPPOSITE end of town from the depot where Pauley, Austin, and Dudley were having their breakfast of biscuits and bacon, Lucas Cain was beginning his own day. His breakfast was beans and *tortillas*, delivered to his room. He would have preferred ham and eggs, but such fare wasn't available, so he made do with what he had. Lucas was just wiping up the last of the beans when Tudway opened his eyes and groaned.

"What the hell?" Tudway said, suddenly realizing that he was tied to the bed. "What is this? What's going on?"

"Good mornin', Jules," Lucas said, moving around so that Tudway could see him. "Want some breakfast?"

"Cain," Tudway said. "You're here?"

"Yep."

"I don't get this," Tudway said. "Where am I anyway? And why am I tied up like this?"

"You're in the Mexican part of town," Lucas said. "This is a room in the cantina."

"I'm in the cantina?"

"Yep."

"How'd I get here?"

"I had a couple of my friends bring you here."

Tudway managed to sit up, though it was with some difficulty.

"No, I don't want any breakfast," he said, answering Lucas's earlier question. "Would you mind telling me how long you plan to keep me?"

"I'm not going to keep you too long," Lucas said. "Just until Cristina, the boy, Mrs. Davenport, and I can catch the afternoon train out of here."

"So that's your game, huh?"

"That's it."

"You're a fool, Cain. You aren't going to leave here. Why, I got more than forty men spread out all through town. Pauley and some of his men are down at the railroad station. You'll never make it."

"If I don't make it, you won't make it," Lucas said.

"What do you mean?"

"When we move down the street toward the depot, I'm going to be holding this double-barreled shotgun right under your chin," Lucas said. He held it up. "And I'll be holding the hammers back with my thumb. If something was to happen to me, like if I was to get shot, why, my thumb would just naturally let go and the hammers would snap shut, firing the gun."

"You're a madman."

"Some folks think that," Lucas agreed.

Suddenly the window exploded in a shower of glass as a bullet came crashing into the room to bury itself in the wall. Lucas dropped to the floor quickly, then crawled over to look out through the window. The street was empty. That in itself was strange, for this was the middle of the morning and the street should have been full of its daily commerce.

"Cain! Cain, I want to talk to you!" Lucas recognized Deke Pauley's voice.

"Damn," Lucas said. "How'd they find out where we were?"

Behind him, Tudway chuckled. "I told you, you wouldn't make it."

"Cain, did you hear me? I want to talk to you!" Pauley shouted again.

"All right," Lucas replied, shouting through the window. "Talk."

"I think you should take a look out in the street. We've got a friend of yours down here."

Lucas raised up to look through the window. He saw Billy Williams, his face badly bruised and bloodied, his hair matted, his clothes torn.

"Recognize this fellow?" Pauley shouted.

"Yes."

"He was real helpful," Pauley said.

"I'm sorry, Mr. Cain," Billy said. "I couldn't help it. They beat it out of me!"

"That's all right, Billy. You helped me when I needed it."

"Yeah, that's what I was gettin' at, Lucas. You see, Billy here had no business helpin' you. Now I'm going to have to show the whole town what's goin' to happen to anyone else who helps you."

"Let the boy go, Pauley."

"Sorry, Lucas. Folks around here need to learn who their friends are," Pauley said. "Austin, Dudley, he's all yours."

Lucas saw two puffs of smoke as two guns fired at Billy. Billy fell face down in the street. From the way he was lying, Lucas knew that he was dead.

"I hope all you good people of Tudway saw that," Pauley shouted. "You good people who are hiding in your houses, under your beds, behind your women's skirts. I hope you saw what happens to people who don't know who their real friends are."

"Pauley! Pauley get me out of here!" Tudway shouted.

"Don't you worry none, Mr. Tudway," Pauley said. "We're goin' to get you out of there. Lucas? Lucas, you got anything to say?"

Lucas had been keeping his eyes on the corner of the building where he had seen a puff of smoke from one of the guns that killed Billy. He knew that whoever was there was going to have to take a peek around the corner eventually, and when he did, Lucas was going to be ready for him. He rested his forearm on the windowsill to help steady his pistol, and he waited.

"Come on, Lucas, what do you say?" Pauley said again. "Why don't you be sensible and turn Tudway and the boy over to us? If you do that now, we'll let you ride out of town."

"You don't expect me to believe that, do you?" Lucas called back.

"Believe what?"

"That you would just let me ride out of town?"

Pauley laughed. "Well, I guess you got that all figured out, haven't you? No, the truth is, I'm afraid it's too late for that. I'm afraid it's going to have to end for you right here."

"How about facing me down?" Lucas called. "Just you and me?"

"You'd like that, wouldn't you?" Pauley shouted back.

"I'm not the only one who would like it," Lucas said. "You know yourself, ever since I arrived, the whole town has been trying to get us together. What do you say? You want to try it?"

All the while Lucas was talking he was keeping his eye on the corner of the building. Then his vigil was rewarded. Lucas saw the brim of a hat appear, then a part of the crown, and finally a sliver of face. Lucas cocked his pistol, aimed, took a breath, and let half of it out. He waited until the head was far enough around the corner for the man in hiding to take a look at what was going on. When the man's eye appeared, Lucas touched the trigger. His pistol barked and the man who was hiding behind the corner suddenly spun around, then fell backward into the alley with a bullet hole just above his eye.

"Pauley! Did you see that?" another voice shouted. "How did he do that?"

"Take it easy, Austin," Pauley said. "Dudley got a little careless, that's all."

"I'm gettin' out of here!" someone shouted.

Lucas saw the flash of a pistol shot, and another bullet came crashing into the room. He pulled away from the window for an instant, then he raised up again and saw that a Winning Hand rider had left his hiding place and was making a mad dash across the street to get to another position. As the cowboy ran, he continued to fire toward Lucas's window.

Lucas fired back once. His bullet caught the cowboy high in the chest and the man pitched forward in mid-run, halfway across the street. He fell across Billy's body, then lay there, perfectly still.

Inexplicably, Pauley began to laugh. He laughed long and hard, then he called out: "Bravo, Lucas, bravo. Two shots, two men dead. You haven't lost your shooting eye, have you?"

"They made it too easy for me," Lucas called back.

"That's the problem when you don't use professionals," Pauley replied. "Austin is the only professional I have left. You whittled us down pretty good."

"I reckon I have," Lucas said.

"But tell me, Lucas. How many bullets do you have left?"

"Enough."

"Really? Enough for all of us?"

"If need be."

"Let's find out," Pauley said. "I'll be back in a little while with a few more friends."

Lucas waited. Ten minutes passed then thirty, then an hour. In all that time he had not heard another word from Pauley, nor had he seen him anywhere on the street.

Lucas left his room and walked down the hall to see Cristina. He found the girl and Roberto sitting calmly on the bed in her room.

"Are you two all right?" Lucas asked.

"*Si*. We heard shooting. They have found us, haven't they?"

"Yes," Lucas said.

"Perhaps we should move to another place."

"Too late," Lucas said. "I'm sure they're downstairs just waiting for us to come down. Come with me. Bring the boy."

Cristina held out her hand and Roberto took it obediently, then followed her as she followed Lucas back down the hall. When they got back into the room, Lucas saw Tudway just beginning to chew on the ropes in an attempt to get free. However, almost as quickly as he started, he jerked his mouth away, spitting and gasping.

Lucas laughed. "What's the matter, Tudway?" Lucas asked. "Don't you like jalapeño?"

"Jalapeño?" Tudway growled. "You coated the ropes with jalapeño?"

"Yeah," Lucas said, checking them to make certain Tudway hadn't loosened them any. "Just a little surprise I had cooked up for you. Did you like it?"

"You are going to pay for this, Cain," Tudway said. "You're going to pay for this."

"Señor Cain. Look out!" Cristina suddenly called, pointing toward the window.

Lucas looked around just in time to see a man precariously balanced on the windowsill just outside the window. He had a pistol in his hand and he was pointing it right at Lucas. Lucas picked up a chair and hurled it through the window. The chair caught the man full in the face and chest, knocking him over backward. The man let out a loud, frightened yell and plunged to the ground about twenty feet below. Lucas hurried over to the window and looked down to see him lying flat on his back, his arms thrown out to either side of his body. Lucas didn't think he was dead, but he would have bet money that the man had a broken back.

There were two people on the roof of a building across the street and they both fired at Lucas. Lucas returned fire. One of the shooters pitched forward clutching his stomach. He tumbled off the roof to join the one Lucas had hit with the chair. Lucas missed the second shooter, but his shot was close enough to send the man scurrying for cover.

"Get down!" Lucas called, but Cristina had already dropped to the floor, taking little Roberto down with her.

"Hey, what about me!" Tudway shouted. "I'm up here on this bed. If I stay up here, I'm going to be right in the line of fire."

"Tell them to quit shooting," Lucas said.

Another volley of bullets came crashing into the room. By now all the glass was gone, but they whipped through the curtains, broke mirrors, and slammed into the wall on the opposite side of the room.

"Quit shooting!" Tudway called.

"I don't think they heard you."

"I said quit shooting!" Tudway called again.

"That's no good," Lucas said. He pushed Tudway's bed over to the window. "Get up here where they can see you and hear you."

"My god! Are you crazy?" Tudway shouted in terror.

"Pauley! Pauley, quit shooting. For God's sake, quit shooting!"

"Hold your fire, men," Pauley said. "Mr. Tudway. Mr. Tudway, are you all right?"

"Yes," Tudway said. "But I won't be if you don't stop this."

"All right, Mr. Tudway, whatever you say," Pauley said. "We'll find some other way to get you out of there."

With the gunfire temporarily silenced, Lucas heard the sound of a distant train whistle. He bent over and started untying Tudway.

"What are you doing?" Tudway asked.

"Hear the train?" Lucas replied. "It's time. We're going down now."

21

"If there is anyone waiting down there, don't shoot!" Tudway yelled from the top of the stairs at the cantina. "For God's sake, don't shoot!"

"All right, let's go," Lucas said, shoving the double barrels of the shotgun under Tudway's chin.

Tudway led the way down the stairs, his head held rigidly erect by the shotgun, his eyes open wide in fear. Lucas was right behind him, holding on to him with his left hand while with his right he held the shotgun. Cristina was just behind Lucas and she was carrying Roberto, who was taking everything in with wide, curious eyes.

Lucas heard someone move down in the barroom of the Cantina.

"I don't know who's down there," Lucas said. "But I have to tell you that my thumbs are already getting tired."

"Stand up!" Tudway shouted. "Stand up so he can see you!"

Two men stood up then, one from behind the bar, the

other from behind an overturned table. Both were carrying guns.

"Throw the guns down on the floor and put your hands up," Lucas demanded.

The two men did as ordered, then, at the nod of his head, walked out into the streets with their hands up.

"Don't shoot!" the two men shouted to the others. "Don't shoot! He'll kill Mr. Tudway!"

Lucas shepherded his little party out into the street, then started them toward the depot. The train whistle that he had heard a moment ago was now much closer, and in fact, not only the whistle could be heard but the chugging, puffing sound of a working steam engine as well.

The cantina was at one end of the street, the depot was at the other. About two hundred yards separated the two structures. As Lucas looked down that two hundred yards he could see Winning Hand riders, some of them on the roofs, some of them behind watering troughs, some of them near the corners of buildings. At the far end of the street, he could see Mrs. Davenport's private car. And standing on the depot platform in front of her car, Lucas saw Mrs. Davenport herself.

"Don't be a fool, Cain," Tudway said. "You'll never make it."

"You had better hope that I do," Lucas said. He jammed the barrel harder against Tudway's chin.

"Don't shoot!" Tudway shouted to his men. "Don't anybody shoot!"

"Tudway, I don't even want them to make me nervous," Lucas said. "Maybe they had better toss their guns into the street."

"Do as he says," Tudway ordered.

One by one, guns began to plop down into the dirt of the street as the little party walked by.

"Cristina, you keep a lookout behind us," Lucas said. "I wouldn't want anyone to get brave after we pass them."

"I will watch," Cristina said.

The train was nearly to the station now, and it sounded its whistle again, then it began breaking with puffs of steam and the screeching sound of metal on metal. Lucas had come one hundred yards, halfway there.

"Vern, no!" Tudway suddenly shouted. He had spotted one of his men just inside the door of the Golden Eagle Saloon, aiming a gun over the top of the batwing doors. "Put your gun down!"

Vern hesitated for a moment, then he tossed his gun through the door.

"Good man, Tudway," Lucas said. "Now tell him to come on outside."

"Come out!" Tudway ordered.

Vern, with his hands up, came outside to join all the other Winning Hand riders. By now there were more than thirty of them, and they were all walking quietly down the street behind Lucas and the others, as if this were a giant parade.

In a way, it was a parade, for the rest of the town was watching from their own positions on the sidewalks and through windows of the homes and businesses. It was a strange, almost bizarre scene being played out in an eerie silence. Slowly, quietly, the parade continued down the street toward the depot.

The train was in the station now, and the conductor stepped off the platform to shout out importantly,

"Tudway! Folks this is Tudway! The train leaves in ten minutes!"

The conductor was surprised to see that the depot was completely deserted. To the small towns in remote parts of the West, the arrival and departure of trains was the most significant event of the day. Such trains were more than mere conveyances for passengers or the means of shipping and receiving goods. They were a physical link with the rest of the country, a visible sign that the townsfolk weren't alone. And yet, as the conductor stepped off to give his clarion call, there was not one citizen of Tudway present to hear him.

"Where is ever—" The conductor stopped speaking when he saw the parade approaching. And at almost the same moment, he saw that the person leading the parade, Jules Tudway, had a shotgun jammed up against his chin. "My god! What's going on here?" he asked.

A few of the passengers on the train, who just happened to be looking out the window at one more tiny stop on their journey, also saw the strange parade coming toward them. Like the conductor, they were instantly curious, and they left the train to get a better look. Within a few moments, the depot platform was crowded, not with the townspeople who normally gathered to watch the passing of the trains, but with the passengers themselves. It was a strange reversal of normality.

The townspeople weren't left out, though. As the parade had passed them on the street they left their vantage points and followed. Now, just at the edge of the depot itself, there were nearly three hundred people gathered, representing most of the town and all the passengers on the train. Even the Mexicans had joined the throng.

Just as Lucas arrived at the depot, Pauley stepped out of the crowd and planted himself in the street right in front of Lucas.

"Well now, you're here," Pauley said, smiling at Lucas. "I have to tell you, Lucas, old friend, I didn't think you would make it this far." The smile left his face. "But this is as far as it goes."

"Out of the way, Pauley," Lucas said. "We've got a train to catch."

"Is that any way to treat an old friend?"

"Out of the way," Lucas said again.

Pauley chuckled. "Or what?" he asked. "Or you'll kill Tudway? Go ahead."

"Pauley!" Tudway shouted. "What are you saying? What are you doing? He means it, can't you see?"

"Oh, I'm sure he does mean it, Mr. Tudway," Pauley replied. "But I mean it too. Go ahead, Lucas. Kill him."

"If he's dead, who pays you?" Lucas asked.

"Oh hell, I don't worry about that," Pauley said. "I was about ready to move on, anyway. But I can't let you go. You understand that, don't you, Lucas? If I let you go, how does that make me look? Why, I'd be the laughingstock of the territory. I'd never get on with anyone else."

Lucas knew that Pauley was right, but all he said was, "That's your problem, Pauley, not mine."

"No," Pauley said easily. "It's your problem too, because we're going to have to deal with it here, now. You said it yourself, Lucas. Everyone wants to see the two of us shoot it out." He smiled and took in the crowd with a wave of his hand. "Look how many people are here. Don't you think we owe them a show?"

"Is that really what you want, Pauley?"

"Yeah, that's really what I want. Now, either kill that

son of a bitch or let him go. I don't care which. And let's you and me settle this thing once and for all."

Lucas eased the hammers down on the shotgun and pulled it away from Tudway's chin. He handed the gun to Cristina.

"Keep an eye on him," he ordered.

"*Si.*"

Lucas turned toward Pauley. The crowd backed away to give them more room.

"You know, all the while you and I were working together, I used to wonder which one of us was the fastest," Deke said.

"Señor!" Cristina suddenly shouted, and right on the heels of her shout came a blast from one of the barrels of the shotgun she was holding. Lucas looked up to see Austin, his chest and neck blood-splattered from the charge of buckshot, pitching forward off the roof of Mrs. Davenport's private car. Pauley had planted him there as a backup.

When Pauley saw that Austin was dead and he was going to have to face Lucas alone, the smile on his face faded. Lucas realized then that the advantage had suddenly passed to him. It might have been, all things being equal, that Pauley was as fast, or perhaps even faster than Lucas. But Pauley had been hoisted by his own petard. He had given himself an edge and now he saw that edge taken away. That left him with self-doubt, and the self-doubt caused him to feel fear, perhaps for the first time in his life. And that fear was mirrored in his eyes and in the nervous tick on the side of his jaw. Pauley's tongue came out to lick his lips.

Lucas waited.

Pauley's hand started for his gun, but Lucas's was out just a heartbeat faster. That heartbeat of time was all the advantage Lucas needed, for he fired first. Pauley caught the ball high in his chest. He fired his own gun then, but it was a convulsive action and the bullet went into the dirt just before he dropped his gun and slapped his hand over his wound. He looked down in surprise as blood squirted through his fingers, turning his shirt bright red. He took two staggering steps toward Lucas.

"How'd you do that?" he asked in surprise. "How'd you get your gun out that fast?" He smiled, then coughed, and flecks of blood came from his mouth. He breathed hard a couple of times. "You have to admit, Lucas, old friend, that we had some good times together."

"Yeah, we did, as long as I didn't have to eat your camp cooking," Lucas replied.

"Come on, you have to admit that I was a genius with bacon and beans."

"You kept us from starving, I'll give you that," Lucas said.

Pauley took a few more steps forward, then fell to his knees. "I, I always figured that I was the fastest," he said in a strained voice.

Lucas didn't reply.

"Lucas?" Pauley said, sticking his hand out toward the man who had once been his friend. He fell forward on his belly, then lay perfectly still.

Someone stepped forward from the crowd, leaned down, and put his hand to Pauley's neck. He looked up at the others.

"He's deader'n a doornail," he said.

"Señor Cain! Look out!" Cristina suddenly shouted. Lucas, who had already returned his pistol to his holster, now spun toward Cristina just in time to see that Tudway had, somehow, jerked the shotgun away from her.

"I'm going to kill you, you son of a bitch!" Tudway shouted, but before he could pull the trigger, even before Lucas could get his own gun out, there was the roar of a gunshot. Lucas saw blood and brain matter explode from the side of Tudway's head as he went down, and he turned to his right to see Mrs. Davenport standing there, holding a huge .58-caliber, single-shot gun, sometimes known as a horse pistol because of the size of ball it fired. The large, heavy ball was devastatingly effective, and in this instance, it had taken away about a third of Tudway's head. There was no need for further examination to determine whether he was dead.

Lucas, who had drawn his pistol but had not fired, now turned to look at the Winning Hand riders. Most of them were now unarmed, having thrown their guns in the street during the walk down here.

"It's all over, men," Lucas said. "You've got nobody left to pay your reward. Is there anyone who wants to keep this going?"

"Not me," a cowboy in the front ranks said. "I've had enough of this."

"Me too," one of the others said.

"Yeah," a third agreed. "I'm gettin' out of here."

One by one, the Winning Hand riders began to walk away. Most of the townspeople returned to their activities as well, though a few of the more morbidly curious hung around a bit longer to look down at the three bodies that had been so recently killed.

"All right, folks," the conductor said to the passengers who had been witness to the drama. "Let's go, get back on the train. We've got a schedule to keep."

"Conductor," Lucas said. "You'll have another car to pick up here."

"Your car, ma'am?" the conductor asked.

"What?" Mrs. Davenport replied. She was still standing in the same spot she had been when she shot Tudway.

"Mrs. Davenport, shall I attach your car to the train?" the conductor asked again.

"Oh, uh, yes," Mrs. Davenport answered in a distracted voice.

"Very good," the conductor replied. "I'll get on it right away."

Mrs. Davenport was still holding the huge, smoking pistol down by her side. Now she raised it up and looked at it for a moment, as if unable to believe what had just happened. Then, with a little cry, she tossed the gun aside. "Oh Lucas," she said. "What have I done?"

"You've saved my life," Lucas said. "And the boy's life, and the girl's, and probably your own."

"But I had to kill a man to do it."

"You should have killed the son of a bitch twenty-five years ago," Lucas said. "Right after he raped you."

Mrs. Davenport looked up in surprise. "You knew?" she asked. "You knew that?"

"I knew he was the boy's grandfather," Lucas said. "And I figured there was no other way he could have been."

"You're a good man, Lucas Cain," Mrs. Davenport said.

"No," Lucas said. "I'm not a good man. But I am good at what I do."

"Well, if you won't take my accolades, will you at least take the money I owe you?"

Lucas smiled. "Yes, ma'am," he said. "That I'll take."

A LOOK AT: THE TENDERFOOT
THE COMPLETE SERIES

Master of the Western adventure, *New York Times* best selling author Robert Vaughan is back with another page turner sure to please Western fans of all ages.

When Turquoise Ranch hand Curly Stevens went into Flagstaff to meet a new employee arriving on the train, his first impression of Rob Barringer is of how big and strong the tenderfoot is. Rob's eagerness to learn and his willingness to take on the most difficult jobs wins everyone over, including ranch foreman Jake Dunford, and Melanie Duford, his beautiful daughter.

Rob is well-educated, and his demeanor and intelligence catches the attention of Melanie, causing him difficulty with ranch manager Lee Garrison, who believes he has an exclusive right to Melanie. Garrison makes life difficult for the ranch hands, and Rob in particular.

When Jake Dunford makes a public accusation that the ranch manager is stealing from the ranch, Garrison reacts by firing everyone, but it is Garrison who is in for a big surprise.

"Vaughan offers readers a chance to hit the trail and not even end up saddle sore."—*Publishers Weekly*

AVAILABLE NOW

ABOUT THE AUTHOR

Robert Vaughan sold his first book when he was nineteen. That was several years and nearly five-hundred books ago. Since then, he has written the novelization for the mini-series Andersonville, as well as wrote, produced, and appeared in the History Channel documentary Vietnam Homecoming.

Vaughan's books have hit the NYT bestseller list seven times. He has won the Spur Award, the Porgie Award in Best Paperback Original, the Western Fictioneers Lifetime Achievement Award, the Readwest President's Award for Excellence in Western Fiction, and is a member of the American Writers Hall of Fame and a Pulitzer Prize nominee.

He is also a retired army officer, helicopter pilot with three tours in Vietnam, who has received the Distinguished Flying Cross, the Purple Heart, The Bronze Star with three oak leaf clusters, the Air Medal for valor with 35 oak leaf clusters, the Army Commendation Medal, the Meritorious Service Medal, and the Vietnamese Cross of Gallantry.

Made in the USA
Las Vegas, NV
06 January 2025